ADVANCE PRAISE FOR
CITY OF LOST SOULS

"The story left me literally glued to the pages. I would say breathless if I didn't want to seem wimpy. The accuracy of the sites and sounds are terrific and the background notes ground the story in fact. Ford takes us on a journey. What fun, what a ride!"

—Jay Grusin, author of *Intelligent Analysis-How to Defeat Uncertainty in High Stakes Decisions*

"City of Lost Souls tells a great detective story evocative of the rich American tradition of noir fiction, forever linked in the popular imagination with Raymond Chandler and Humphrey Bogart. But in this case the setting is 1930s China and the protagonist is Jack Ford, cynical and dogged, and following his own code in a world gone mad. Tapping four decades as a top CIA Sinologist, Petersen draws the reader into the fantastical cruelties and beauties that was interwar Shanghai. Readers will never be able to visit that time and place, now lost forever. But a glimpse is possible through reading this book."

—Dennis Wilder, former Director for China on the U.S. National Security Council

"If you want a classic PI story reminiscent of Sam Spade / Mickey Spillane — tough, no-nonsense PI's set in the Far East with realistic characters, settings and plot, then this is for you. The author's description of 1930s Shanghai, with its politics, social strata and complex interplay and intrigue, is exceptionally insightful and the story and action sequences clearly reflect Petersen's in-depth knowledge of Chinese history, society, culture and traditions, and Shanghai in particular."
— Michael Fallon, retired senior CIA intelligence officer

"Martin Petersen has crafted an excellent thriller taking the reader back in time to that fascinating city, Shanghai in the 1930s. Petersen's book fired my imagination, put me in that city and made me feel I was witnessing the events firsthand. His book is well researched, and his knowledge of the region gives City of Lost Souls a depth and richness lacking in far too many books. When I finished reading, I found myself wishing for more. I hope this is the first of many books by Martin Petersen."
— David Cariens, retired CIA officer and author of
A Question of Accountability The Murder of Angela Dales

CITY OF LOST SOULS

A JACK FORD SHANGHAI MYSTERY

Martin Petersen

EARNSHAW
BOOKS

City of Lost Souls

By Martin Petersen

ISBN-13: 978-988-8843-86-2

© 2024 Martin Petersen

FICTION

EB219

All rights reserved. No part of this book may be reproduced in material form, by any means, whether graphic, electronic, mechanical or other, including photocopying or information storage, in whole or in part. May not be used to prepare other publications without written permission from the publisher except in the case of brief quotations embodied in critical articles or reviews. For information contact info@earnshawbooks.com

Published in Hong Kong by Earnshaw Books Ltd.

For L.E. and U.W, who encouraged me to write.

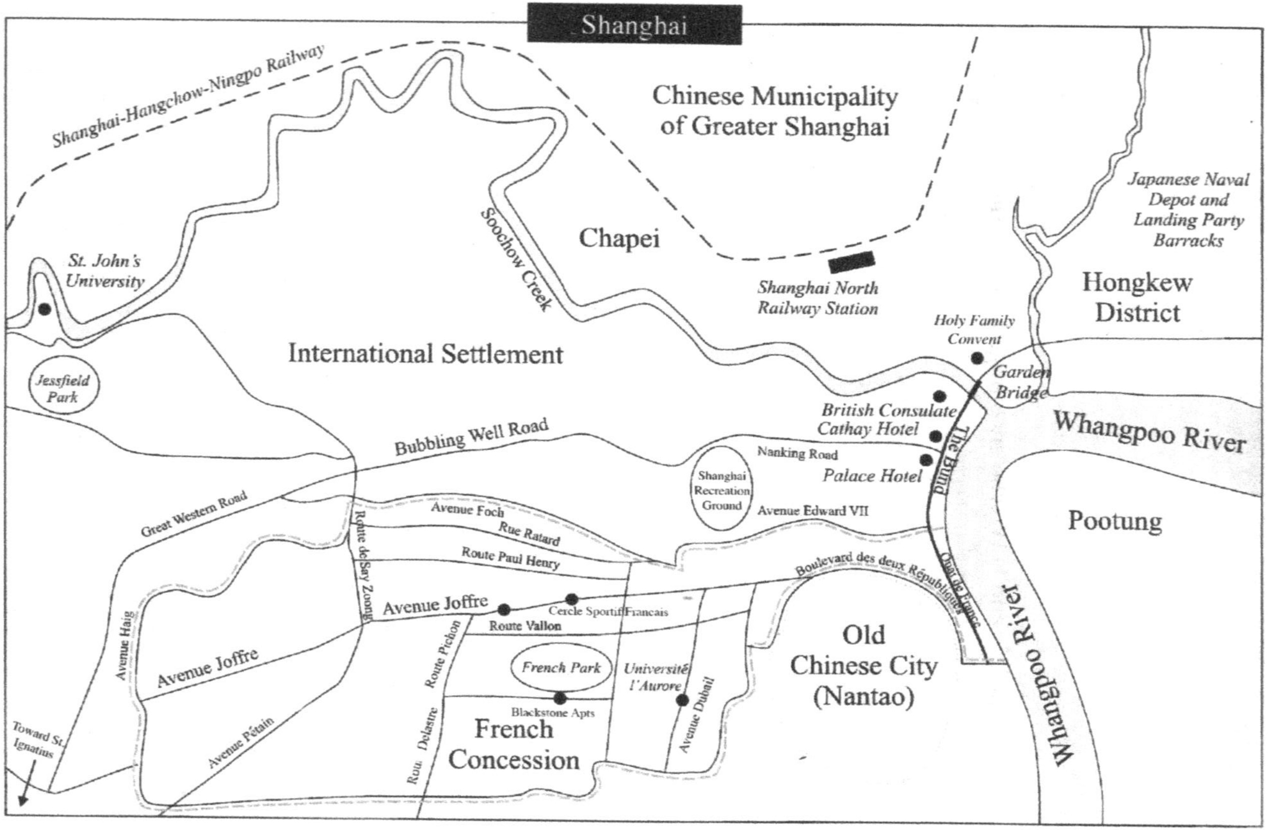
Shanghai
Shanghai-Hangchow-Ningpo Railway
Chinese Municipality of Greater Shanghai
Japanese Naval Depot and Landing Party Barracks
Chapei
Soochow Creek
St. John's University
Shanghai North Railway Station
Hongkew District
Holy Family Convent
International Settlement
Jessfield Park
Garden Bridge
British Consulate
Cathay Hotel
Whangpoo River
Bubbling Well Road
Nanking Road
Palace Hotel
The Bund
Shanghai Recreation Ground
Avenue Edward VII
Pootung
Great Western Road
Avenue Foch
Rue Ratard
Route de Say Zoong
Route Paul Henry
Boulevard des deux Républiques
Quai de France
Avenue Joffre
Cercle Sportif Francais
Route Vallon
Old Chinese City (Nantao)
Avenue Haig
Avenue Joffre
Route Pichon
French Park
Université l'Aurore
Avenue Dubail
Blackstone Apts
Whangpoo River
Toward St. Ignatius
Avenue Pétain
Rou Delastre
French Concession

"A city of forty-eight-story skyscrapers built upon twenty-four layers of hell." — playwright Xia Yan

August 1971 California

"How old are you?"

"Excuse me?"

"I said, how old are you? It's a simple question."

"I'm twenty-four."

"And remind me again what you want with me?"

"I'm a PhD candidate in Chinese history at Berkeley, and I am researching the Japanese attack on Shanghai in '32. Father Chin suggested I interview you. He said you were there, and probably have some unique insights on events."

"Father Chin, he's a Jesuit, right? Worked with Father Jacquinot?"

"That's right."

"You've never been there, Shanghai, I mean?"

"No. You can't travel there if you are an American. What I want to know is what it was like in the run up to the actual start of fighting."

"What was it like? Like nothing you will ever know."

CHAPTER ONE
Thursday, January 7, 1932

You smell it before you see it. Your liner enters the Yangtze, and you get a whiff of land, but it is only the silt of the great river. You sail up the Yangtze to the Whangpoo and then you really smell it. Sweat, ginger, garbage, opium, gin, and money. Especially money. Past the shipyards, wharfs, and factories on the right bank and the tiny vegetable plots in Pootung on the left. Then, the city starts to come into view. The crowded areas of Yangtszepoo, Hongkew, and Chapei and then the granite towers of commerce and power that make up The Bund.

Shanghai was a free city. It belonged to no one. There was an International Settlement that was self-governing and a corrupt French Concession that was in bed with the top Chinese gangsters. No visas needed. Just get off the boat. And the flotsam and jetsam of the world washed up here. There were rich Western elites, Sephardic merchant princes, adventurers, missionaries, do-gooders, and those fleeing someone or something.

And of course, Chinese, some richer than Croesus but most barely staying alive. The average Chinese was treated with disdain at best by the foreign community and often worse by

CITY OF LOST SOULS

his Chinese superiors. Both city services and charitable societies were taxed to the maximum in just sweeping up the corpses on the street every morning of those who perished overnight from cold or hunger or just the exhaustion of trying to stay alive.

Shanghai was my home, and I loved it despite everything. I'd seen a lot of China. A lot to like, and a lot not to like. I had been there for almost twenty years in 1932. I was sixteen and a young Marine when I arrived as part of the detachment sent to Peking after the collapse of the last dynasty to protect American interests and prevent a repeat of the Boxer Rebellion. I stayed on after my enlistment like many other China Marines who had nothing to go home to and eventually made my way south to this city of refuge.

1931 had been a rough year for Shanghai. Crime was bad and Chinese gangsters and elements of the Nationalist Chinese government were battling for control of the opium market. The Chinese communists were on the run, but Moscow and its agents were active. A cholera epidemic in the countryside and widespread floods had filled the city with refugees, clogging the old Chinese quarter and spilling over into the Western-controlled parts of the city. Beggars were everywhere and getting bolder.

In September the Japanese military had staged an incident in Manchuria and grabbed control of most of Northeast China. The world stood by and did nothing, and now the militarists had their eyes on Shanghai, the key to controlling the Yangtze River Valley and all of Central China. Chinese workers were on strike in Japanese factories and students were organizing boycotts of Japanese goods. Tokyo responded with demands that the Shanghai Municipal Council put an end to the protests. Some in the Chinese leadership were gunning for a fight with the Japanese and had even ordered the 19th Route Army to take up defensive positions west of the Concessions.

MARTIN PETERSEN

In January 1932 my city was on the edge of an explosion. I didn't think it could get much worse, and then she walked into my life.

———∽∾∽———

Bone tired and half hung over from the night before, I stood at the window of my office in the Missions Building staring at a woman on the street. She was tallish and had auburn hair. A stylist raincoat hung on her shoulders, and she was smoking a cigarette, something women in those days rarely did on the streets. I thought she must be strong willed or just indifferent to the conventions of the day. She seemed to be undecided. She kept glancing at a slip of paper in her hand and the front of the building. Then she was gone.

A few minutes later, Peter stuck his head into my inner office and said, "Mr Ford, there is a lady here to see you. Miss Constance Baker-Kerr. She says she got your name from the manager of Astor House."

"Baker-Kerr?" My face must have betrayed my feelings about upper class Brits because he smiled a little. "Show her in, Peter."

It was the women from the street. She walked into my inner office and stood about six feet from my desk, as if she was uncertain about what to do or whether she even wanted to be here. She turned and watched Peter leave the room and close the door.

She smelled clean. That was the first thing I noticed, and the English tweeds. The raincoat was draped over her arm and a pair of kid gloves were tightly gripped in one hand.

"Please sit down, Miss Baker-Kerr, or is it Mrs?"

"Miss, I'm not married." She glanced back at the door as she sat down.

"He's quite tall, isn't he? Your boy, I mean," she said with a bit of surprise in her voice.

"He is not a servant. He is my assistant, and his ancestral home is Peking. Northern Chinese are taller."

There must have been a bit of an edge in my voice because she pulled back a bit. I could see she was nervous and debating whether she should have come. As she sat down, she reached into her bag for a cigarette not thinking or bothering to ask if she might smoke. I leaned across my desk to light her cigarette and inhaled soap and powder.

Her auburn hair was set off by deep blue eyes. I put her in her early 30s. Her hands were small, which seemed at odds with the rest of her. She was buttoned up tight from throat to floor, but you could tell she had a full figure, and she had that pale skin I always associated with northern climes. She was not a classic beauty with her soft triangular face and small chin, but there was something about her that drew your attention and suggested strength. She later told me she was an "acquired taste."

"So, how can I assist you, Miss Baker-Kerr? What brings you to Shanghai, and to me?"

"I'm looking for my brother. He was supposed to meet me when I arrived Monday, but he seems to have disappeared, and I'm very worried. I don't know what to do. I know no one here, and the manager of Astor House suggested that I contact you." It all came out in a gush.

"Please try to relax. If I am going to help you, I'll need to know your story. So, take a deep breath, compose yourself, and tell me why you and your brother are in Shanghai."

"It is rather complex, I'm afraid."

The hand with the cigarette shook slightly.

"Just tell it how best you can." I pulled a cigar from the silver holder in my breast pocket, leaned back, and lit it with heavy lighter on my desk.

"It really begins with my late father. He was a China scholar specializing in early Buddhist texts. I have assisted in his work since I was a young girl, cataloging materials, typing, managing correspondence, that sort of thing. My father was a member of Sir Aurel Stein's expeditions to Chinese Turkistan. Perhaps you've heard of him?"

"Stein? I know of him, but that's all."

"Well, he is quite accomplished, and my father worked with him. My father was with him in 1907 when Sir Aurel discovered the "Caves of the Thousand Buddhas" and the Diamond Sutra. It's one of the first printed texts. Of course, he wasn't knighted at that time. That came later."

I sensed she was getting off track. "Please just focus on your story, Miss Baker-Kerr." She took a long drag on her cigarette and then snuffed it out in the crystal ashtray on the corner of my desk.

"Yes, of course. He, Sir Aurel not my father, he brought back cases and cases of manuscripts and relics. It amounted to nearly 40,000 items. My father was helping with the translations and exploitation of the materials. My father was also part of his second expedition in 1913, but he had a falling out with Sir Aurel and went on to make a number of discoveries on his own. He sent these back to England, and I worked on cataloging these relics and putting his notes in order until earlier this year. My father contracted a fever in 1914 on his way home and he died in China and is buried in Kashgar. My mother passed away in 1918 during the flu epidemic.

"So, there is just my younger brother Robert and me now. Robert accepted a position with Jardine Matheson here in late 1928, and he suggested I join him in Shanghai. I have become quite expert in early Buddhist texts myself from helping my father in his work, and I thought I might also be able to edit my father's notes and get them published here. He so much wanted his work recognized."

"Your father passed some time ago, but you just now decided to come halfway around the world?" I could see she detected the note of skepticism in my voice.

"I was working with a don at Oxford on my father's materials and that has come to an end. My parents being gone, there was nothing to keep me in England."

She was averting her eyes and twisting her gloves. This wasn't making sense somehow and I suspected that I was getting just part of the story, but I encouraged her to go on. "And your brother was supposed to meet you and he failed to show up?"

"Yes. I was not too surprised that he was not at the dock. Robin, my brother's name is Robert, but we have always called him Robin. Robin is young and impetuous and a bit naïve. He is not always responsible, so I was irritated but not terribly surprised when he failed to meet me."

I nodded and encouraged her to continue.

"I had reservations at Astor House, so I went there. I called his office, but I was told no one has seen him for weeks. That made me worried. He can be so impulsive. I've been more mother to him than sister at times, what with our mother's passing.

She fumbled in her bag for another cigarette and lit it herself with a gold lighter. Well, she has money, I thought, judging by the tweed suit and the lighter.

"I'm sorry. I'm a bit upset. After I called his office, I talked to the manager at Astor House, and he suggested that I talk to you. He said the hotel has used you in the past and that you are honest and very capable. He said you have lived here for some time and had good connections across the city. So, I took the chance of calling on you without an appointment. Mr Ford, I do hope you can help me locate my brother. I hope nothing has happened to him."

"I'll have to thank Alan. He's the manager you spoke to. Actually, he gave me a call and told me you might come to see me. I do have good connections, not only across the city but also across the various social strata that make up Shanghai. I've lived here for almost twenty years, and I consider it home. The Ford Agency is discreet. It's honest and it can operate across the city's many communities. Those are three qualities that are hard to find together in Shanghai. What do you know about Shanghai, Miss Baker-Kerr? You need to have some appreciation of the challenges I face if you retain me."

"Only what I've read...and heard. East meets West? Rather gay and rather sinful."

"Your description is accurate if more than a little understated. This is a city that is going to explode if the tensions between the Chinese and the Japanese continue to escalate. The Japanese military has set its eyes on dominating East Asia. That means controlling China and getting rid of the Westerners. They took a big bite out of China last September and now they are nibbling around Shanghai. Students have been protesting here, and there have been clashes between them and the ronin."

"Ronin? I'm sorry, I am not familiar with the term."

"Japanese gangsters and thugs. They're paid by the Japanese military to tear down anti-Japanese posters, rough up Chinese protesters, break windows in shops boycotting Japanese goods. The situation is getting worse by the day. In fact, I strongly suggest that you check out of Astor House and check into the Cathay Hotel on The Bund. Astor House is next to little Tokyo and the Cathay is on this side of Soochow Creek, which is where you want to be because it will be safer if things get worse."

She looked a bit stunned but nodded, "if you say so."

"Miss Baker-Kerr, you need to understand how this city

works or doesn't work because it's not England and I need you to understand the challenges we face in finding your brother, if he is truly missing. This city, well, think of it as a cocktail. One-part bad French champagne, two-parts Brit and American whisky, and a large helping of Japanese saki that is threatening to overpower the drink. Garnish with Chinese patriots, warlords, gangsters like the Green Gang, Jewish merchant princes, white Russian refugees, assorted crooks and fast money operators. Serve in a large Chinese goblet and you have Shanghai. Only the ingredients don't mix. At least not easily and not unless there is a reason to."

She looked at me as if she were trying to make up her mind if I was kidding or at least exaggerating. "That is very confusing."

"Which is why you need me, Miss Baker-Kerr. Shanghailanders, have a well-developed sense of honor and no sense of shame. This city is about money and the fear of losing it. Everybody is going back to somewhere else and the object for most is to make as much money as possible as quickly as possible and then get out. The missionaries and the stateless persons are exceptions. They at least see the Chinese. To the others, John Chinaman is invisible, or at least they act like he is."

"Aren't you being awfully cynical? And what about you, Mr Ford?"

"I've been here a long time, Miss Baker-Kerr. It is my home. I'm not going back to anywhere. I know this city like few do. I can move among its centers of power and layers of society, although the taipans and compradors avoid me unless they need me for something.

"As you say, it is confusing and challenging. You bet. Which is why finding your brother and what happened to him will not be easy. And again, why you need me. And I might not even be able to do it. I don't want to frighten you or dishearten you. We'll probably find out that he has a girl or something. You said he can be impulsive and irresponsible. But I'd be misleading you if I didn't tell you that there is also the possibility that something has befallen him. Understand?"

She nodded and said, "Yes, and I would like to retain you. I have funds in the Hongkong & Shanghai Bank."

"Fine. Peter will prepare a contract for you to review and sign. I do things by the book. I play straight and I expect my clients to be straight with me."

I took a pad of paper from my desk drawer and opened my fountain pen and asked her to describe her brother. She couldn't tell me much that helped. He was tall, had red hair, and of course was "impetuous". She knew nothing about his life in Shanghai. She could tell me nothing about friends or clubs or even interests. She knew he worked in the insurance section of Jardine's and had a flat in the Villa Apartments in the French Concession. He must have been doing well because those flats were upscale. I asked her to go through his letters and look for names of people and places. She did have a picture of him, which she promised to give me when we met the next day.

"We haven't discussed my fee. I get US$25 or the equivalent a day plus expenses. I also require a US$100 retainer that goes against the daily rate. I will be honest with you, Miss Baker-Kerr. Based on what you have told me, this could be expensive, and I cannot guarantee results. I will work it as long as you like, however. Is this acceptable?"

She took a deep breath, nodded, put out her cigarette, and in a low voice said yes.

"Then I'll have Peter draw up the contract for you and we can sign it when we meet tomorrow. Peter will take you to Astor House to get your things, and then he'll take you to the Cathay Hotel, which is very new and very nice. Victor Sassoon has built himself quite a pleasure palace on The Bund.

"I suggest we start by checking your brother's flat. It is near mine, actually. I'll have Peter pick you up in the morning and bring you to my place and we'll go to the Villa Apartments together. Say 10:00 a.m. tomorrow?"

She nodded, then got up, and I buzzed Peter in the outer office to get her.

After they had gone, the phone rang. It was Alan who said he wanted to pass on some information about my new client, and that it would be best if we talked in person. I told him I could be there late that afternoon.

I wrote a note to Peter asking him to check with our contacts in the Shanghai Municipal Police and the French Gendarmerie, and if they had nothing, call the hospitals and check the morgues. Then I grabbed my grey fedora with the silk hatband and the snap brim and headed out the door.

CHAPTER TWO
Thursday, January 7

Alan Mowbray was not the manager of Astor House but the head of security. He was a former London Bobbie who had come East after the Great War. He had good contacts and a cop's nose for things that were not quite right.

I took a rickshaw and headed up The Bund toward Garden Bridge and the north bank of Soochow Creek where it joins the Whangpoo River. Astor House sat on the corner. Originally this had been the American Concession, but the American and British Concessions merged in 1863 to form the International Settlement. The French flirted with the idea of joining but, as usual, went their own way in the end. The Russian, German, and Japanese Consulates were cheek by jowl near Astor House, a real collection of bad actors. The US Consulate had been there too but moved to Foochow Road in the 1920s.

Astor House was the first grand hotel in Shanghai and for a long time had been the best. It was stately if a bit of a rabbit warren. I waved at the deskman and made my way down a side corridor to Alan's office in the back. His door was open, and I walked in. He stood to greet me, stuck out a large hand—he was a big man—and said, "Hello, Jack."

"Hi, Alan. Thank you for sending Miss Baker-Kerr my way. I have taken her case. Might not amount to much, but she is a bit of a looker. So, thank you again," and I smiled broadly at him.

He chuckled a bit and waved me toward a small table and chairs and took the seat opposite me. "Thanks for coming by. It may be nothing, but I thought I ought to share some information about Miss Baker-Kerr with you."

"Something wrong?"

"Well, yes and no. Let me explain what happened and you can tell me if I'm being overly cautious."

Alan took a deep breath and started. "She, Baker-Kerr, arrived Tuesday afternoon. She had sailed from England via the Canal, Bombay, Singapore, and Hong Kong. Nothing unusual about that. When she booked her room here before sailing, however, she also requested that we inform her brother. That struck me as a bit odd, but apparently, she had wired him about her planned arrival but hadn't heard anything back. We left messages at Jardine Matheson and at his flat and forgot about it."

I asked when she had booked the room and when she had sailed.

"I'll have to check if you want the precise dates, but it was early November. Anyway, she arrived on schedule, checked in, and then asked if her brother had left any messages for her. She said he was not at the dock as expected. I got all this from the head clerk at our front desk. We had no messages. When her brother failed to call the next day, she approached me, and I sent her to you. She checked out of here just before noon."

He took another breath. "Now the odd part. This afternoon a Mr Tachibana inquired at the front desk if Miss Baker-Kerr was in. Our man at the desk told Mr Tachibana she had checked out and left no forwarding address. We knew where she went, of course, because she told the desk man in case her brother suddenly turned up. But we never give out that kind of information to strangers.

"I called you, Jack, because Tachibana just struck this old Bobbie as being not quite right. His card had only his name and a phone number, but I know he is associated with the Japanese mission here and in fact, is an officer in the Imperial Navy. Why isn't that on his cards? And why is the Japanese Navy interested in Miss Baker-Kerr? Did she mention that she had Japanese friends in Shanghai?"

I shook my head. "No, in fact she stressed that she knew no one here, other than her brother. And she seems at a complete loss about his life here. I agree it seems odd, and that may be all it is. See what you can find out about Tachibana? I'll do some checking, too. She told me some of her history, but nothing in it touched on Japan. I think she is holding something back. Thank you for passing this on, and I'd appreciate anything else you can discover."

"No problem, Jack. Happy to do it. The Japs have become awfully pushy of late. Their Marines are all over the northern part of the city, and I know they are bankrolling if not directing those ronin thugs who are causing so much trouble."

It was a just little after 5:00 p.m. and I considered my options. A drink seemed like the logical choice and then dinner, either at home or perhaps out. I belonged to the American Club, which was a few blocks away. Fortune Magazine once described its lobby as reminiscent of a well-decorated hospital. I decided I needed something a tad more decadent. I engaged a rickshaw and told the coolie to take me to the Cercle Sportif Francais in the French Concession.

CITY OF LOST SOULS

The Cercle Sportif Francais was one of Shanghai's true delights. It was a fabulous building of what looked like white marble but was actually painted brick and mortar. Unlike the snooty Shanghai Club (where they even ironed the newspapers), the French Club welcomed women, successful Chinese (as guests), and Shanghailanders of almost every nationality. It was only five years old in 1932 and was built on the site of the old German Country Club. The Great War wasn't the only thing the Hun lost, although the Germans were back now and in some force. The club featured the biggest ballroom in Shanghai plus a rooftop terrace for dancing. It had the best billiards room, the largest swimming pool, a great smoking room with a superior selection of cigars and cognacs, and of course, restaurants serving great food. And being French, beautiful women were always in view.

I made my way to the horseshoe-shaped bar. I had ordered a Bombay Sapphire Martini straight up with a twist and was admiring the plaster nudes on the columns when I heard my name called. It was Carl Crow, an old friend who had been in Shanghai longer than I had. He had a successful public relations business and was a major supporter of the Generalissimo and Chinese interests. Carl was the rare exception to the general Shanghai contempt for the Nationalists in particular, and, the Chinese more generally.

He waved me over. Sitting with him were two of the better-known personalities in the city. The respected one was Stirling Fessenden, the Secretary-General of the Shanghai Municipal Council, effectively the mayor. He had round glasses and chubby cheeks and he always reminded me of "Cuddles" Sakall, the actor. Stirling had that same cheerful personality, and the politician's touch for making friends and small talk. The notorious one was Captain Etienne Fiori, the very corrupt Frenchtown Chief of Police.

"Sit down, Jack," Carl said. "We were just discussing the situation with the Japanese and the Nationalists. I think you know these gentlemen."

"I do, indeed. Mr Mayor, Captain." I nodded to both.

"I say Jack, you know I'm Secretary-General. There has never been a 'mayor'."

"I still think of you as Mayor, Stirling, as does everyone else." He chuckled satisfactorily.

Fiori picked up the conversation where it had apparently left off. "I see your government, Jack, says it will not recognize Tokyo's takeover of Manchuria. What do you think of that?"

"Well, it's not 'my government', Captain, and I don't care what Washington thinks. But I do believe we are headed for trouble. I know the US Marines are setting up positions along Soochow Creek opposite the Japanese in Chapei."

"I don't care what the heathens do," Fiori said with his usual condescending tone, "as long as they keep it outside the Concessions. I am only concerned about the French Concession. It might be best for us all if the Japanese taught the Nationalist rabble a lesson or two."

"Come, come, Captain. Surely you realize violence would be bad for us all, including French business interests." Fessenden puffed out his cheeks a bit and went on. "The Japanese Consul General has been in my office almost every day since December complaining about the Chinese boycott of Japanese goods and the Nationalist newspapers in the Settlement. And the clashes are becoming more frequent and more violent. The Shanghai Municipal Police had to break up another anti-Japanese demonstration by Chinese students on Monday, and this time a police officer was hurt."

"Both sides seem to be gearing up for fight," Crow offered. "The KMT has moved three divisions of Cantonese soldiers into the area and formed them into the 19th Route Army under General Tsai and he hates the Japanese. He won't back down from a fight if it comes to that. And the Japanese Marines are patrolling more aggressively, too."

"I know Tsai, or I should say I know of him," I offered. "I saw him in action when Chiang marched north against the warlords. He knows his business."

"Well, gentlemen, things are quiet in Frenchtown," Fiori observed with an air of Gallic superiority.

I rose to the bait, if that was what it was. "Well, I guess it helps to keep things quiet when you put the head of the Green Gang on the French Municipal Council and his partner in crime is Chief of Chinese Detectives."

"Mr Ford, the secret to efficient policing is to control those things you can, and to seek help from others in controlling those things you cannot. Please excuse me, gentlemen. I have a dinner engagement with some very influential members of the larger Chinese community."

He got up, bowed slightly, and left.

I looked at Carl and Stirling. "Must be time to collect his cut of the opium and vice traffic." They smiled.

"Care to join us for dinner, Jack? Stirling and I were about the to try one of the restaurants in the Club."

"No thank you, Carl. I think I'll head home."

January weather in Shanghai can be rainy and cold, but the temperature was in the forties, so I decided to walk the few blocks south to my flat on Rue Lafayette. Lao Wu greeted me at my door, and as always, he was wearing the long black silk robe with white cuffs that he had worn as a minor official in the Manchu Dynasty. He had fled to Shanghai with his family when the

Northern Warlords took power. Father Jacquinot had introduced us, and I hired him to manage my life outside the office. I really didn't know much about him. When he wasn't looking after me, he smoked, drank tea, and practiced his calligraphy. Peter was his son, and Lao Wu, Peter, his wife, and their little daughter all lived in the servants' quarters behind my kitchen.

"You catchee chow-chow, Massa?" Peter spoke perfect English, but his father had only a few words and we generally communicated in pidgin. I thanked him in my halting Mandarin and told him no, I did not want anything. I asked if Peter was back, and Lao Wu went to get him. I made myself a martini, lit a cigar, and plopped down in my favorite chair next to the radio.

Peter came in and told me that he got Miss Baker-Kerr safely checked in at the Cathay Hotel. He said that the police had no information and his inquiries at the hospitals and morgues had turned up no one matching our client's brother. I reminded him to pick up Miss Baker-Kerr at 10:00 a.m. and he went off to bed.

I tuned the radio to XMHA, and caught the news, which was more of the same: clashes between ronin and the Chinese, Japanese complaints to Fessenden about press articles "offensive to the Imperial household," and more labor unrest in Japanese textile mills. I feel asleep in my chair.

CHAPTER THREE
Friday, January 8

Peter had Miss Baker-Kerr at my flat a little after 10:00 a.m. I showed her to the dining area where Lao Wu had laid out coffee, tea, and pastries. She looked softer, dressed in a yellow skirt and pale blouse that brought out the blue in her eyes.

"Miss Baker-Kerr, I had my assistant check with the police. They have no information about your brother. I also had Peter check the hospitals and the morgues, and there was no one answering to Robert's name or matching his description. That is a positive."

"Mr Ford, my Christian name is Constance, but my friends call me Connie. Baker-Kerr gets to be a mouthful after a time. Please use my first name, especially since this is likely to take some time." She smiled broadly and I did the same. The morning light flattered her.

"Well, Connie, call me Jack, then. And you are right. This is likely to take some time. It is nice to rule out hospitals and worse, but…well, it deepens the mystery. Something may have befallen your brother, or he does not wish to be found."

I could see Peter was trying to get my attention. I asked

Connie to excuse me for a moment, and Peter and I went into my library.

"What's up, Peter?"

"I am almost certain we were being followed. I noticed a black sedan fall in behind us when I pulled away from the Cathay. It stayed a few cars back but made every turn we did. I did not try to lose it or be evasive. I did not want the driver to know he had been made. When I pulled up here, it went past There were two men, Oriental, in the front seat, and possibly a third man in the back. I am not sure."

"Not sure, right?" Peter nodded. "Okay, take the car and drive to the office. See if you are followed. Don't try to lose them. If they are tailing us, I don't want them to suspect we know. Connie and I will walk to Robin's flat, and we'll meet you back at the office, probably mid-afternoon. Also, follow up with Alan. See if he has learned anything more about Mr Tachibana."

Connie was sipping tea. I asked her if she remembered to bring a picture of Robin, and if she had gone through his letters for names of friends or places he liked. She passed me a photo. It showed the two of them sitting at a large table in a garden. They both looked happy. She said his letters were few and contained no names of people or places.

I pocketed the photo, quietly glad that Connie was in it too. "I'll return this. The Villa Apartments are not far. We can walk if you wouldn't mind. The weather is pleasant, and I needed to send Peter to tend to some urgent business. Taxis and rickshaws are scarce in this neighborhood."

What I didn't tell her was that I wanted to see if we were being shadowed, and that would be easier to determine if we were on foot.

The Villa Apartments were only a few blocks north and east of my place. We strolled leisurely stopping to look at the French

Park and the newer buildings. If we were being followed, I couldn't spot it. They were either not there or very good.

———∽∽———

The concierge of the Villa Apartments was a bamboo Brit of the first order. That's an American who affects an English accent and manners, generally with a double helping of condescension. He stonewalled when I asked if Robin was in and refused to say when he had last seen him, citing the exclusiveness of the Villa Apartments and the residents' expectation that their privacy would be respected. I was about to grab him by the lapels when Connie put on her best smile and with an air that one-upped the man told him that as Mr Baker-Kerr's sister she had every right to inquire as to his well-being. And she feared that he may be ill and in need of help, especially as the Villa's respect for their residents' privacy seemed to prevent them from noting anything about their residents or their doings.

Her smile turned icy, and it had a visible impact on the concierge. "We would just like to check his flat and you, of course, are free to come with us. You do have a master key?"

We took the elevator to Robin's third-floor flat. I knocked and when there was no answer, I grabbed the key from the concierge and opened the door. I told him to wait in the doorway, adding I knew he would want to respect Mr Baker-Kerr's privacy. I walked immediately to the servants' quarters at the back of the flat. No one was there and more important, there were no personal effects of the Number One boy.

I walked back to the concierge. "No one else has been in the flat, correct?"

"Of course not!"

"Not even servants? How many did Mr Baker-Kerr have?"

"He had a Number One boy who lived in. There may have

been others. I don't know."

"Has anyone been around inquiring after Mr Baker-Kerr?"

"No."

"That includes Orientals? Servants, perhaps, Chinese or Japanese business associates?"

"No one, until you."

"Okay. It's clear that Mr Baker-Kerr has not been here for several days, perhaps longer. He didn't mention to you or others on your staff that he was going on holiday? Didn't ask you or anyone to gather mail or feed the fish or water the plants?"

"No!" He was becoming increasingly indignant. There were no plants or fish. Robin didn't seem to be spending much time in the flat. There was nothing personal about the place, no pictures or books or trinkets. There were some matchbooks from various nightclubs. I quietly pocketed them.

"I'm just going to take a quick look around to see if he left a note or something that might indicate where he has gone. Connie, please check the desk and see if there is a diary or schedule of some sort."

I went into the bedroom and looked in the closet. The clothes were pushed around and there was a shotgun case and shotgun in the corner. One of the nightstand drawers was slightly ajar. I opened it and there was nothing in it except for a half empty box of pistol cartridges. No pistol, however. I did a quick check of the bath. No shaving kit.

I joined Connie in the living area. "Does Robin like to hunt or shoot?"

"Well, yes. He is quite a good shot. Mostly skeet, although we did hunt grouse in Scotland sometimes. Why?"

"His shotgun is in the closet is all. Did he own a pistol? I found a box of cartridges in the nightstand."

"I don't know. Perhaps he did."

"I'll check out the skeet club at the Recreation Grounds. See if anyone there knows anything. Anything in the desk?"

"No. Just some writing paper. There is a notepad, and it had my planned arrival information on it. I recognize Robin's handwriting. There are some magazines and newspapers. The papers are all from early December. I don't think he has been here in some time, Jack." Worry was in her voice, and she was having trouble controlling it.

I cut her off. I didn't want her to say anything more in front of the concierge. "We mustn't take up any more of the gentleman's time. I'm sure he is busy."

Connie turned toward the concierge and said with ice in her voice, "And, please do tell me if you hear anything. I am staying at the Cathay Hotel. I can be reached there or though Mr Ford."

I gave him my card and we left.

Peter was waiting for us in the office when we got back to the Mission's Building. Peter said he had checked with some of the Chinese personnel at Jardine's. They told him that Robin had not been in the office since early December, but he had mentioned he might travel in the area over the holidays. Peter had also checked with Alan, who had nothing more to offer about Tachibana, other than he was certainly a naval officer and had been in and out of China since before The Great War.

I asked Connie to make herself comfortable in my inner office while I spoke to Peter privately.

"Were you followed?" I asked.

"I do not think so. I drove back here slowly as you directed, and a car, perhaps the same one as before, pulled out initially but broke off after a few blocks."

I thought about this for a moment. "If you were followed

this morning, then they were interested in your passenger and not you or me. We walked to the Villa, and I detected no surveillance, but I couldn't be sure. Peter, I believe someone has been through Robin's flat. Things were moved around a bit, so it was not obvious, but some drawers were ajar. Also, I think Robin took a pistol with him or someone removed it. There was a half box of shells but no gun. And no sign of the Number One boy. His quarters in the back are clean, like he left permanently, not temporarily. I want you to find the Number One boy and see what he knows."

Peter was my assistant for a number of reasons. He spoke English, Mandarin, and the Shanghai dialect, could drive, handle a firearm, and pose, when necessary, as an ordinary Chinese and go places where I couldn't. This was one of those times I needed his skills.

"Go chat up the servants at the Villa and see if you can learn the identity of Robin's Number One boy and where he might be. Also ask if they have seen any strangers around his flat."

I returned to Connie with a cup of tea for her and a cup of coffee for me. She was seated in the chair near my desk. I took my cup and moved to a corner near the inner door. Things weren't adding up. Her brother knew she was coming and she said they were close, so why didn't he meet her or at least leave word? And why would he tell people he would be traveling if his sister was coming? I felt I didn't have the full story of why she was in Shanghai. I hardened my voice.

"What did you see in the flat?" I asked.

"I don't think Robin has been there for some time and I'm more worried now than before."

"I think you're right about his being gone. Did Robin mention anything about taking time off or traveling?"

The edge in my voice must have registered with her because

her answers became shorter and her brow was lined. "Do you have any idea why he would travel when he knew you were coming? Or where he would want to go?"

"No. Like I said, his letters really didn't say much about his activities and certainly not about his plans."

I took a deep breath and stepped in closer. "Here's what I think. Robin hasn't been in the flat for weeks. The Number One boy hasn't been there either, which is unusual if Robin planned to come back in a few days. I believe the flat was searched. I don't know by whom or why. I found pistol cartridges in the nightstand but no gun. So, Robin took it because he felt he might need it, or whoever searched the flat did. And, the Japanese are awfully interested in you, a Mr Tachibana in particular."

Her eyes widened and the lines in her brow deepened. "And here's what I suspect. I suspect the Japs are also interested in you because they believe you know where Robin is. Do you?" It was my interrogation voice.

"But I don't. And I've never met a Mr Tachibana. I told you I don't know any Japanese," she said with irritation in her voice.

"Peter thinks you were tailed to my flat this morning. He said he can't be sure, but he thinks so, and Peter is usually right. I don't know who tailed you. The Japs are at the top of the list, but if the Japs are interested in you, then maybe the Nationalists are interested in what the Japs are interested in. And that doesn't rule out the communists or the Green Gang or Shanghai's run-of-the-mill criminals."

"This is very confusing and frightening, Jack."

"It sure is, Miss Baker-Kerr." She was a taken aback by my use of her last name. "What is it that you are not telling me? Why did you really come to Shanghai? I'll dump you right now if you are not going to be straight with me."

I could see her stiffen and her eyes glistened. I thought she was playing me for a sucker. Don't fall for it, don't fall for it, I thought. But I realized, too, I was beginning to care more than I should.

There was a bit of temper in her voice, which gave way to a plea. "Don't abandon me. I have no one else to help me. It is all so strange and frightening."

I sat down in the chair next to her and said more softly, "Time to come clean, Connie. There is something more going on here and you are not telling me. Tell me. Tell me what this is all about."

She drew a breath, and I could see her chest heave. "It is like I said, Jack, I came to be with my brother and finish my father's work. That's true but, but..."

"But there's more, right? What about your father? He seems to be part of this."

"You have to understand that my father loved China and especially loved its culture and religions. He wanted to be a university don, study China and write, especially about the beginnings of Buddhism in China, how it traveled from its Indian origins to China and then to the rest of Asia. But he didn't have the right credentials." She said credentials like it was a swear word.

"He didn't have an Oxford or Cambridge degree, so the university post he ached for, literally ached for, was never going to happen. So, he did what he thought was the next best thing. He signed on with Sir Aurel and made at least two long trips to Central Asia with him. He was with him in 1907 when Sir Aurel made his great haul at the Caves of a Thousand Buddhas and again a few years later.

"Stein shipped back thousands of Buddhist objects and manuscripts, and my father, who was quite good at classical Chinese and Sanskrit, helped him translate part of the find. He also helped catalogue the findings and date the manuscripts. But my father had a falling out with Stein. I don't know why or precisely when. I do know that he left the expedition, did some exploring on his own, and was in Kashgar in 1914.

"Mother was still alive. We received a cable from Calcutta in October 1914 that my father had died of fever in Kashgar. The British Consul in Kashgar, a George Macartney, was the source of the information. The cable said father had been buried in the consular cemetery, and that Macartney was forwarding to my mother my father's effects and papers, including a large chest containing Chinese and Sanskrit scrolls and documents."

"How did the Raj know where to send the cable?"

"Well, my father was fairly well known in British Asian circles. The cable actually came via the colonial office. I remember my mother remarking on that, and it was brought to us by a government official who said he was with the colonial office."

"Was he?"

"I have no reason to believe otherwise, and my father's papers and artifacts arrived some months later. There was a letter with them. In it he said that he had made what he thought was a significant find, and that the scrolls and papers were only part of it. He said the most important items were two small scrolls and a fragment of a document. The two scrolls pertained to the Kaifeng Jews and the fragment seemed to be a part of the Gospel of St. Mark in Greek and classical Chinese. Father's letter said that he couldn't risk losing them, so he gave them to a man named Ding Mu, a Chinese Muslim who was his assistant and lived in Yin-ch'uan in Ninghsia. He said that if anything happened to him, we should contact Ding Mu."

"Doesn't it strike you as odd what your father did? Ship most of the stuff home but leaving the most important items with a servant? It sounds like your father feared for his life or at least was afraid of someone or something. Was the letter dated or was a place or name given? Kashgar?"

"I don't know. There was no date or place on the letter. I do think he was concerned because he said he wanted his work to be known and acknowledged, and that if he could not do it, he hoped others would complete it. Perhaps he was already very ill. I was in my teens when this happened, and I vowed that I would study Chinese and carry on my father's work."

I sat back trying to take all this in and how it might possibly be connected to events. "Where are your father's papers now? Still in England?"

"No, I shipped them on ahead of me to a Mr Chu, who is an assistant curator at the Oriental Library here. It has a very large collection of rare documents. Chu knew my father and I hope to get him to help me prepare my father's work for publication."

"Why do that? You said you were working on his papers with the help of a don. Why take the chance of shipping them half away around the world? I still don't understand why you came here when you could have finished your work in England. It's more comfortable and certainly safer."

She looked away.

"Connie, what are you not telling me? I'm trying to see if there is a connection between all this and what is happening now."

"I couldn't stay in England." She paused and it came out in a rush. "There was a scandal. I was involved…emotionally…with the don, and it was discovered, or he confessed to his wife." She sniffled and with a weak laugh said, "I hardly look like 'the other woman', do I? In any case, there was nothing left to keep me there. My brother was here, and I wanted to finish my father's work. So, that's the sordid truth."

"Who knows about the special papers?"

"Only my brother, and my late mother, of course. I never told anyone, not even the don."

I wasn't sure this was the full story. It didn't explain the

Japanese, and an affair didn't seem to be enough to move halfway around the world to someplace she had no ties to except a brother now missing.

"I don't know how all this fits together or even if it does, but I do think you are in some danger. I'm going to get you a bodyguard. His name is Mikhail. He's a White Russian. He's very quiet, very big, and very good.

He will accompany you when you go out if I am not with you, and frankly, I think it best if I operate on my own for now."

"Is this really necessary? Maybe I should move into my brother's flat. In case he comes back?"

I decided to change tactics. I shifted back to a softer tone.

"No, Connie," using her first name again. "The flat was entered by someone, and maybe I'm being overly cautious, but Shanghai can be a dangerous town even for respectable people. Kidnappings for ransom are not unusual, and there are the Japanese asking about you and the tail from the hotel. It just doesn't make sense unless they, probably the Japanese, want something from you.

"The Cathay Hotel is public. Sassoon doesn't put up with nonsense unless it's of his own making, and that is generally just parties and drinking. The security team is very good there, and I'll tell them to keep a special eye on you. Mikhail will be with you when you leave the hotel. We'll get to the bottom of this, and we'll find Robin."

I don't know why—it wasn't in my good cop bad cop catalogue—but I put my arm around her, and she put her head on my shoulder and wiped the wetness from her eyes.

"Let me show you a bit of Shanghai's nightlife. Something pleasant. Dinner tomorrow and a few of the better nightclubs and cabarets. We'll find your brother, but you need to start to make a life here if you plan to stay."

CHAPTER FOUR
Saturday-Sunday, January 9-10

Saturday is my day for errands, and since Lao Wu handles almost everything, it generally comes down to a visit to Caldbeck, MacGregor & Co. to replenish my liquor cabinet and then to H. H. Bodemeyer for cigars. I tried a pipe once but I couldn't keep it lit. So these days I favored Romeo y Julieta No. 2s. I later learned they were also Churchill's favorites. The only thing I had in common with the great man. I also dropped in at C. N. Gray and Company, my tailor, and had a second fitting for a new suit. I've always been fussy about my clothes.

Traffic in Shanghai was exactly what you would expect, chaotic, especially around Nanking Road where it becomes Bubbling Well Road at the Recreation Grounds. There are autos of every make and description, rickshaws, wheelbarrows, carts, and of course, lots and lots of people, who walk however and wherever they want. During the work week, Peter drives me but, on the weekend, I like to drive.

In 1932 I had a green and tan 1930 Packard Roadster with white walls and leather trim. I loved that car. New, it cost over $2,000, but I bought it for a song from a French official who thought it best to leave Shanghai in a hurry, especially after the Green Gang delivered an elaborate coffin to his home. Big Ears Tu was anything but subtle.

I replayed my conversation with Alan as I made my way through the traffic back down Thibet Road to Frenchtown. I apparently had two mysteries now. Where is Robin and why were the Japanese interested in Connie? I made a mental note to check back with Alan to see if he had learned anything more.

My flat is in the Blackstone Apartments, a new set of flats on Rue Lafayette. Mine was on the second floor and at this time of the year, I could see a bit of the French Park from my living room window. Rue Lafayette is mostly apartment complexes, a few Consulates, and quiet. Plane trees give shade in the summer but also block my view of the French Park. I had a nodding acquaintance with my neighbors but didn't know them or care to. I had converted one bedroom into a library where I had the radio, my favorite chair, a liquor cabinet, humidor, and my books. I spent most of my time in that room.

Also in there was Saudade, my large white cockatoo who always greeted me with a welcoming screech, a bobbing head, and a loud, "he lo, he lo, he lo." She wouldn't stop until I gave her a grape or small piece of Chinese melon.

She was a gift from Father Jacquinot who told me I needed at least one thing in my life to connect with on an emotional level. And he named her.

Lao Wu told me lunch was ready in the dining room. I thanked him, kissed Saudade on the beak, and began thinking about my promise to show Connie a bit of Shanghai nightlife. I told Lao Wu that I would need Peter to drive us that evening.

I met Connie in the lobby of the Cathay Hotel at 7:00 p.m. She was wearing a long, light green evening gown that was cinched at the waist and had a décolleté that intrigued but did not advertise.

"You look lovely," I told her. "I have a lime green and tan Packard Roadster that is the perfect complement to your gown. Unfortunately, it only has two seats and Peter will be driving us, so we will use my Ford sedan instead. I hope you don't mind that I am in a suit and not a dinner jacket." I realized I was beginning to ramble, and I stopped.

"You clean up quite nicely," and she smiled broadly. "I hope I'm dressed appropriately. I heard Shanghai is a stylish town."

"It is and you're perfect. I thought we would start here with cocktails and dinner then hit Frenchtown for the cabarets and dancing. If that is all right? We'll start at the top and work our way down to some of the...the more interesting places that give Shanghai its reputation. Nothing untoward, of course." I was babbling again. She was certainly beginning to have an effect on me.

"I'm quite the big girl, Jack. I think I can handle it, and it sounds delightful." She offered her arm, and I took it.

We took the elevator to the Rooftop Garden at the top of the Cathay Hotel. We were led to a small table by the corner windows in the bar area. The Whangpoo River with its warships, freighters, sampans, and great ocean liners reflected the lights of The Bund. The Cathay was in the elbow of the river's gentle bend. When facing the river to our left was the Bank of China and farther along the British Consulate Grounds, the Public Gardens, Garden Bridge, Astor House, and the narrow streets of the Yangtszepoo District. To the right was the Palace Hotel, the Customs House, and the Quai de France, the French section of The Bund. Pootung with its small vegetable plots was dark except for the scattered glow of the tiny oil lamps and cooking fires that dotted that swampy ground.

"Oh, Jack, this is lovely. I never imagined this."

"It is impressive," thinking to myself, 'if you are a Shanghailander and not a poor Chinese.'

Our cocktails arrived and we toasted one another. Moments later Carl and Mrs Crow approached our table.

"Good evening, Jack. Might I ask who this lovely young lady is, and will you introduce us?"

"Mr and Mrs Crow, please meet Miss Constance Baker-Kerr, who has just arrived in Shanghai and plans on spending some time here. Connie, please meet Carl and Mrs Crow. Carl is one of Shanghai's most eminent residents. He runs a very successful public relations firm and is a strong supporter of the Nationalists and the Chinese people. Please join us, Carl."

"Thank you, we will," he said and immediately turned his full attention to Connie and that gown. "Miss Baker-Kerr, what brings you to the mysterious East?"

"Please call me Connie. All my friends do, and I do hope we will be friends. My brother works for Jardine Matheson, so I am here visiting him. I am also editing my late father's journals, which I hope to have published. He worked with Sir Aurel Stein and was an authority on early Buddhist Texts."

"Connie, you must call me Carl, everyone does. And, you have truly taken me by surprise. You are Sydney Baker-Kerr's daughter, then?" Carl said with genuine delight. "I know of your father, of course, and I actually met him once or twice when he passed through Shanghai so long ago. A great friend of China, I must say. I am so delighted to meet you. You said your late father. I did not know that he had passed. I am terribly sorry. Please accept my condolences."

"Thank you, Carl. My father passed some years ago. It was quite sudden, and I have been working with a Cambridge don to put his papers in order and make a record of his life's work. I've done all I can in England, and I hope to finish the project here. I sent my father's papers on ahead and they are being kept for me at the Oriental Library of the Commercial Press."

Carl seemed truly excited. "Well, excellent. Do you read and speak Chinese then?"

"I can read some, but my father's work focused on classical Chinese and Buddhist sutras. The Cambridge don was a major help with that. I hope that someone at the Oriental Library can advise me."

"Well, I can be of use there," he said with enthusiasm. "Let me make some introductions for you. The Oriental Library and the Shanghai branch of the Royal Asiatic Society are places to start. You must meet Arthur Sowerby. And you'll need a publisher. There is the Commercial Press but also Kelly and Walsh. I can be of help there too. Oh, this is exciting."

Thankfully—as far as I was concerned—the manager of the Tower Restaurant, came over to tell us our table was ready. We bid the Crows a good evening, I signed the chit, and walked to our table in the hotel's elegant dining room.

"Jack, not that it is my business, but you didn't pay for our drinks."

"I did Connie. I signed a chit. In the better places, it is easier for Shanghailanders to just sign a chit. At the end of the month, you settle the debt with the shroff who comes around and collects. Welsh, on one of those, and the word gets around immediately, and every door is closed to you. Serious stuff," I said with a smile.

"My, I certainly have a great deal to learn about your city, Mr Ford," she said returning my smile.

We finished our dinner a little before nine and headed for the Cinderella Club where Whitey Smith's band was playing. Whitey had come to Shanghai just after The Great War. He played in a number of clubs before opening the Cinderella in Frenchtown in '30 or '31. Whitey specialized in the ballroom music that the Chinese loved to dance to. Connie and I took a couple of whirls on the floor. We moved well together, I thought.

After a drink, we headed to the Canidrome to hear Buck Clayton and the Harlem Gentlemen, a hotter group. The Canidrome was quite something. It featured dog racing, Jai Alai, boxing, a cabaret, and a large ballroom. Henry Morriss, who published the *North-China Daily News*, never did anything in half-measures, and he certainly pulled out all the stops when he built the place. Buck and the Gentlemen were resplendent in their white double-breasted suits, and they played the kind of jazz Duke Ellington played. Connie and I mostly listened but did dance to "Between the Devil and the Deep Blue Sea," which seemed appropriate somehow.

We then headed to the International Settlement to catch the midnight show at the Majestic, a high-class cabaret that featured the dancing of Joe and Nellie Farren. Nellie was the draw. She was trim and her costumes left little to the imagination. She was doing her Aztec number that night dressed in feathers and not much else. Connie seemed to be enjoying herself.

Things are only getting underway at midnight in Shanghai, and we left shortly before one a.m. to take in a couple of the taxi dancing spots. We headed back toward Frenchtown and dropped in at the Ambassador, on the border between the two parts of the city. It was famous for, or notorious for, its "hostesses". There were more than a hundred of them, mainly White Russians. They were not quite at the end of their line because there were several more drops down before you hit Jukong Alley or the Trenches.

Connie seemed fascinated by the place. "Who are these women?" she asked.

I said, "Many are coasters or Sonyas, Shanghai slang for

women of, well, easy virtue."

"You must think I am a delicate flower, Jack. I am not unaware of such things," she said giving me a smile.

"They are not all prostitutes to be certain, but they do tend to be down on their luck. They wash up here because you don't need a visa to get in. The employment opportunities are limited, especially if you are White Russian, so they do what they can. In some circles in Shanghai there is a real prejudice against Eurasians, although they are a major part of the white-collar staff of big corporations and trading houses and they couldn't survive without them. A young man like Robin can ruin himself with gambling and liquor but that takes time. Break an unwritten rule here and you'll find yourself dead socially.

"Do you think that is what has happened to Robin?" she asked concerned.

"No, and I didn't mean to imply that. The social etiquette is complex, and a lot of things are tolerated, but there are some hard lines too. Money can fix some things, but not everything."

We watched the scene for a bit lingering over yet another cocktail. I felt her hand on my arm and asked if she wanted to call it a night. She said no, and I suggested a step down. We headed to the Black Cat on Avenue du Roi Albert.

The Black Cat was known for its White Russian taxi dancers who aggressively hustled drinks. It was also a cop haunt, not the senior inspectors but the rank and file of the French Constabulary. And sure enough there were a number of familiar faces in the joint, including some from the Shanghai Municipal Police Riot Squad. It wasn't a rough crowd, certainly not by Shanghai standards, but it was quite a step down from where we had started the evening. The liquor too.

It was well past two now and I suggested that we ask Peter to drive us back to the Cathay Hotel. I told her I would point out a couple of the more notorious addresses on our way. Connie agreed. Peter drove us up Avenue du Roi Albert to Avenue Joffre, where we turned toward The Bund skirting the old Chinese walled city on our right. I had Peter slow at Route Admiral Courbet and pointed to number 43.

"That little building, Connie, houses an opium den and a gambling operation. The Green Gang controls it and the French leave it alone for that reason. We're also close to Rue Chu Pao San. It's better known locally as Blood Alley. Lots of bars and saltwater sisters, cheap prostitutes. We'll slow and you can take a peek down the street. It's frequented mostly by merchant marines and various navies. It's close to the river and it's the sort of place that made Shanghai a verb in the old days. Still a good place to get rolled or knifed."

Her eyes strained to see down the alley as we crept past, the sound of music and arguing came through the window. We turned left onto The Bund, and in a few minutes were in front of the Cathay. I walked Connie to the elevator, and just before she stepped in, she turned and kissed me lightly on the lips. "I had a wonderful evening," she whispered. The elevator doors closed, and I stood there not sure what to think.

―――∞―――

Every few weeks on Sunday I drive out to St. Ignatius to visit the Mother Superior at the convent and leave something for the children in the orphanage there. After my night on the town with Connie—and I was still trying to determine what that small kiss meant—I decided a drive would help clear my head.

I've always had a complicated relationship with the Church. Not with God, heaven help me, but with the institution. On the one hand, I have to be deeply thankful for what they did for me. I was an orphan too. My name is Ford because that was the make of the automobile that dropped me off with the sisters. On the other hand, I left as soon as I could and joined the Marines, one thing led to another and I ended up in Shanghai.

Most of the orphans are Chinese or Eurasian and my heart goes out to them. I know what it is to be one of them. Shanghai is a cruel city, but there are good people like Dr. Anne Fearn who ministered to the poor and founded a school for the maimed, halt, and blind. The Door of Hope rescues children from brothels, and the orphanages in the city have a drawer where families can leave a baby. You pull the drawer, lay the baby in, shove the drawer shut, and ring the bell. The river patrol still fishes dead children out of Soochow Creek every morning. More and more so recently what with the influx of refugees from the interior.

I parked beside the cathedral and walked over to the convent. The Mother Superior knew I was coming and was waiting for me. It was cold and the wind was picking up, but we sat outside on a small bench. I had brought some clothing for the children and passed a red envelope with a contribution to the Mother Superior. She did as she always did, thanked me sincerely, inquired after my physical and spiritual health, and encouraged me to start attending Mass again. I did as I always did. I nodded, asked about the children, and promised to return. I left unstated whether that was to the orphanage, the Church, or both.

I walked back to where I parked and looked up at St. Ignatius with its soaring twin spires. I just stood there and took it in for a minute. I drove the fancy Packard out there and I drove the fancy Packard back, and like every time, I left a little piece of myself there.

CHAPTER FIVE
Monday, January 11

On Mondays I had a standing handball game with Father Robert Jacquinot de Besange at Aurora University where he taught English and literature. Father Jacquinot was the most remarkable man I ever knew, and probably the bravest man I ever met. He was a tall man with a noble nose and was very much the Jesuit. He had a squared off beard that once had been reddish but now was silver. He may have been in his fifties, but he was fit and regularly wiped the deck with me in our handball games despite having just one hand. He lost most of his right arm when the fireworks he was making in the Aurora chemistry lab exploded. It did not slow him down. He was the chaplain to the Shanghai Volunteer Corps and a deadly shot with the Webley .455 he sometimes secreted in his cassock.

When Chiang Kai-shek launched his coup against the left wing of his party in March 1927, it was a bloodbath, and the Holy Family Convent and Orphanage on North Honan Road sat right in the middle of some of the heaviest fighting. There were 400 nuns there and more than 200 children. Father Jacquinot with two senior British officials set out to rescue them. He thought he had a guarantee of safe passage from the warring factions, but some troops stopped them, and the Brits were turned back. Father Jacquinot went on alone despite a shrapnel cut to his head and a bayonet wound to his good hand. When he got to the Convent, there were over a thousand men, women, and children taking shelter, and somehow he was able to use a lull in the fighting to get them all back across the Garden Bridge to safety. The Chinese called him "Old Do Things."

Because western names are so hard for Chinese to pronounce, most Westerners adopt a Chinese version of their last name. Father Jacquinot's was Jao. Mine was Fu Te. It was given to me by an old man who wrote letters for illiterate Chinese, carved fancy ivory chops for visitors, and told fortunes besides coming up with transliterations of western names. Fu Te was "very lucky name," he assured me. "It means Virtuous Teacher." This amused Father Jacquinot no end, and he favored a pun, Fu Fei, which translated basically as "bandit Buddha." It comes closer to capturing your conflicted character, he insisted.

After our game, we retired to his office as usual for a couple of bottles of beer he had brewed. Fireworks were not the only thing he could cook. "Father, you get around as much if not more than anyone I know. How do you read the situation with the Japanese and the Nationalists? Are we in for it?"

"Jack, I am worried. I think the Japanese are brewing for a fight and General Tsai and his troops are more than willing to give them one. The ronin are running wild in Chapei, and I am worried about our parish there and the convent. The year 1927 was bad, but that was over quickly. I think this will be much worse, if it happens."

"If there is fighting, do you think it will spill over into the Concessions?"

"Who knows? I know Fessenden and the Municipal Council

are plenty concerned, and your Marines have taken up positions along the creek. It won't take much to ignite the powder."

I took a sip of my beer. "I see things the same way. I have a client, a Miss Baker-Kerr, new to town. I had her move from Astor House to the Cathay Hotel because I think it's better to be on this side of the creek. Her brother has gone missing. You wouldn't know Robert Baker-Kerr, would you? He has red hair. His friends sometimes call him Robin or Red Robin, I think."

"No, the name means nothing to me. Do you think something serious has happened to him or is he just catting around town?"

"I can't say for sure, but I think the former is more likely than the latter. He was supposed to meet his sister when she arrived, but he didn't show. I guess he is a bit irresponsible, but the Japs have been sniffing around his sister and I think his flat was searched. Their father was a China scholar of sorts, Sydney Baker-Kerr. Did you know him?'

"No, I did not know him, but I knew of him. He was one of the fellows who worked with Sir Aurel Stein. He passed through here on occasion. I bumped into him at the Shanghai Municipal Police Headquarters once. He was coming out of the political section. Odd place to see him, actually. I think he spent most of his time at the Oriental Library. Can you talk about the case?"

I must have looked hesitant because he said, "Now come Jack. Think of this office as just an extension of the confessional, and it's probably as close as you've been to one in ages. I can keep a secret."

"You know it's not that. I just don't know what I'm dealing with. Pieces but no pattern yet." I took a breath and let it out. "This Sydney Baker-Kerr was with Stein when he made his big find at the Caves of a Thousand Buddhas. The two had a falling out, not at all clear why, and Baker-Kerr went off on his own. He apparently found some potentially groundbreaking documents that he entrusted to a Chinese assistant for safe keeping. Baker-Kerr then dies in Kashgar after contracting a fever. His papers are shipped home to his daughter, my client, who is preparing them for publication, so she says. That's it in a nutshell."

"I take it the 'groundbreaking' finds were not in the artifacts shipped home."

"No. Presumably, they are still with the assistant. That is another thing that doesn't make sense to me. My client had the other papers shipped here, and they are in the care of a Mr Chu at the Oriental Library."

He opened two more beers. "What's the nature of the groundbreaking relics, if I may ask?"

"According to his daughter, they relate to some Chinese Jews..."

Father interrupted me. There was a mixture of surprise and excitement in his voice, "The Kaifeng Jews?"

"Yes, that's right. Kaifeng Jews and that's not all. He also found what he believed to be a fragment of the Gospel of St. Mark in Greek but with Chinese annotations. Who are the Kaifeng Jews anyway?"

Father Jacquinot took a long pull on his beer. "Well, that would be something if it turns out to be the case. Not a lot is known about the origins of the Kaifeng Jews. They are Chinese and have been in the Kaifeng area for maybe a thousand years. Kaifeng is on the old silk route. The Kaifeng Jews probably were Jews from Persia or that area. They settled in Kaifeng and intermarried with the local Chinese.

"Long before Marco Polo, there was a steady stream of travelers from India and Central Asia to China, especially during the Tang and Song Dynasties. Roman coins have been found in China and Chinese porcelain and silks made it to Europe but ideas moved along the route too, not just goods. Buddhism came to China from India, so it's not improbable that Jewish and early Christian artifacts also made the journey east.

"This would be a major find if true. Lots of people would be interested in it. The Pure Land Buddhist Sect, for instance, would be interested. Count Otani, who runs a monastery in Kyoto, made two or three trips to the same area as Stein looking for early Buddhist documents and artifacts. Maybe the Japanese are interested in your client because he found something they want, or they want to know what he found? Just an idea."

"Well, that makes as much sense as anything at the moment, Father. I've got two mysteries, I think. Where's the brother and what are the Japanese up to with my client. Thanks for the beer."

I decided to walk back to my flat despite the dropping temperatures and a cold wind. I replayed in my head parts of the conversation with Father Jacquinot as I walked toward the Blackstone.

The good Father said two things that struck me as significant, although I couldn't put my finger on why. He said he once ran into Sydney Baker-Kerr at police headquarters. What the hell was he doing there? And in the political section? He might visit the police for any reason, but the political section, Special Branch, perhaps?

The other comment was the off-hand suggestion that perhaps Baker-Kerr had found something the Japanese wanted. But what? Ancient Buddhist texts? Or had Baker-Kerr learned something that Tokyo wanted to keep quiet? That might explain an interest in the old man, but why the apparent interest in the children? I felt I still didn't have Connie's full story and recognized that I needed to do more checking on her.

Just pieces. A jigsaw puzzle without a box top. I was at my

flat. Lao Wu told me dinner would be ready soon. I went to my library and poured myself a drink. Saudade's "he lo he lo he lo" greeted me and I took her off her perch, put her on my shoulder and gave her a bit of melon. I sat in my favorite chair and looked Saudade in the eye. "What do you think I should do," I asked her. She cocked her head and spread her wings as if to say, "You're supposed to be the smart one."

I took a small pad from the table next to the chair and made a list: see if Peter has located Robin's Number One boy; make inquiries about Robin at the rifle range; talk to my contacts in the SMP about Sydney Baker-Kerr and about Connie, too; find someone who knows about the Stein and other excursions into Central Asia and Chinese Turkistan; and call on Connie to give her an update.

Pretty much in that order, but especially see Connie. Maybe move her up the list

CHAPTER SIX
Tuesday, January 12, 1932

I met Connie the next day for a quick breakfast at the Cathay Hotel and I told her about my plan to ask about Robin at the rifle range. I did not tell her what Father Jacquinot had said about a possible link between her father and the police. I figured it would only increase her concerns, and I wanted to know more first, just in case she was still holding something back. I was finding myself more attracted to her all the time, but I still did not fully trust her, and my history with women was not good.

After breakfast I walked to my office in the Missions Building where Peter was waiting.

"I've got a lead on Robin's Number One boy," he said. "His name is Lo. I spent yesterday chatting up the boys at the Villa Apartments. It took some time and a few coppers, but a cook told me that Robin had given Lo a month off with salary. He said the servant had family in the old Chinese City, and for a few more coppers he could arrange to have someone show me where. This contact is supposed to meet us near the entrance to Yu's Garden in the old city at 11:00 a.m."

"How do we recognize him?"

"We don't. He recognizes us. I suspect the mysterious someone is actually the cook who was shaking me down for a few more coins. I guess we'll see."

I took off my good overcoat and put on a filthy trench coat and changed my Florsheims for a pair of rubber soled boots. You really didn't want to wear your best when you went into the old walled city, but there was nothing I could do about my suit. Peter was in a long black scholar's gown. He looked like the proprietor of small store. He would fit in. I would stand out but there was nothing I could do about that.

"Are you carrying?" I asked. He showed me the Webley that was in the pocket of his gown. I took my .45 from the desk and slipped it into the side pocket of my trench coat.

We took a rickshaw to the old north gate at Honan Road and Boulevard des Deux Republiques. The city wall was mostly gone. It had been built when Shanghai was just a fishing village and was being continually raided by Japanese pirates. When the foreigners demanded Concessions after the Opium War, the Chinese granted them the worthless, swampy land outside the city wall. Well, that's history for you. The best real estate deal since the Dutch bought Manhattan, I guess.

The old city is an assault on the senses, especially after the relatively clean and pleasant neighborhoods of Frenchtown. There was every kind of conveyance and absolutely no traffic pattern. Just jostle and push. Rickshaws, hand trucks, wheelbarrows, push carts selling steamed buns and noodles. There were street barbers cutting hair and cleaning wax out of ears. There were professional letter writers. Little stores, many no bigger than a doorway, selling daily needs. Men carrying live ducks in baskets or on poles, pig heads, and fish in dirty tanks.

And people. Lots of people. Many in rags, refugees from the floods and the fighting in the countryside. Toddlers in split pants defecating and urinating anywhere and everywhere.

The odors were almost overwhelming. Offal, cooking oil, human waste, incense, sweat. And the noise was continual. Crying children, men and women hocking and spitting, godawful Chinese opera, clacking mahjong tiles, and arguments.

Peter and I passed under the old stone arch of the north gate into this chaos. Yu's Garden and the Willow Pattern Teahouse were just a couple of blocks past the gate. They were must-see stops for foreign visitors to Shanghai so they could say they had seen the real China when they got home. There was an open area between the teahouse and the garden that was filled with stalls selling food and trinkets. Jugglers, street acrobats, and beggars all competed for copper coins tossed by the visitors. The Willow Pattern Teahouse sat in a pond and was reached by the Nine Dragon Bridge, which zigged and zagged above the water because evil spirits can only travel in a straight line. The entrance to Yu's Garden, a lovely walled compound built by a Ming Dynasty official, was off to the side and was open to visitors for a fee.

He spotted us, and as Peter suspected, it was the cook from the Villa Apartments. In a thick Shanghai dialect, he explained to Peter that we needed to follow him, and he set off at a quick pace.

Stepping into the old city was not stepping back in time. It was stepping into an awful present. We moved down Ju Kung Ka Road past Zao Char Road, and then we were in a side alley. I had no idea where we were or even the direction we were heading. It was a series of twists and turns, each offshoot of an alley narrower than the last until there was barely a shoulder's width between wooden structures with tin awnings and roofs.

Everywhere dripping water, some from laundry hung on poles, some probably from emptied chamber pots. Wires stretched between structures stealing electricity from the Shanghai Power

MARTIN PETERSEN

Company. It was dark even at noon and probably even dark in the summer. There was so little space for light to reach the ground. We passed a damp wall with dozens of joss sticks in it. Some geomancer must have decided this was a lucky spot, a place to come and make a wish and an offering for heaven knows what.

We took another turn and rats scurried. They were everywhere and they were aggressive. People were intruding in their environment. I heard a loud bang, and I froze. I tapped the .45 in my pocket and I could see Peter up ahead doing the same with the Webley. He said, "What do you think that was?"

"Don't know, but not a gun. Just keep moving." The cook was hurrying ahead.

I paused and looked through an open door at a man who could not have been ninety pounds. He was lying on his side on a wooden platform staring at an old woman who was quickly kneading a gummy, dark substance with two needles. Opium. I watched her as she heated the substance, and it changed color from dark brown to tan. She loaded the pill into a long pipe, lit it, and gave it to the man. He took it all in one deep intake of smoke, and a blue haze seeped from his mouth and the air had a sickening sweet smell.

The foreign visitors see Chinese everywhere, in the streets, as clerks in shops, as waiters in restaurants, as rickshaw pullers, and if the city isn't fast enough, as bodies in the street or in the creek. But they have no idea what life is like for the Chinese or how they feel about you.

I quickly caught up with Peter, who was holding up his hand. "We're here." The cook scampered away and was gone with a turn down another alley. I had no idea how we would find our way out.

It was a structure like all the others, a couple of stories but more substantial than most. A young girl sat in the window of a first-floor room with thermoses of hot water for sale. There were no stoves or heat in the building, so the inhabitants, you could hardly call them residents, bought boiled water from the girl to make tea. Cooking was in the street between the buildings.

As we approached the entrance, I could see a woman washing noodles that had spilled into the street. There were tears in her eyes. This was the meal for the day undoubtedly and she had spilled it in the gutter. Now she was doing her best to salvage what she could. At least her rice bowl wasn't broken. That could mean starvation.

"The cook says Lo lives on the top floor in the back," Peter said. We started up the stairs. The building had been divided and divided again into rooms and then into just sleeping spaces that were little more than four feet by five feet. At the top there were two rooms. One had been divided by partitions into four sleeping spaces and there was an emaciated rickshaw puller in one of them. Peter asked if he was Lo, but he just shook his head and pointed to the other room.

The door was ajar. The room was empty except for a sleeping mat and a chamber pot. There was blood on the wall and two teeth on the floor. Peter went back to the skin-and-bones man and asked where Lo was, but the man just shook his head.

We went downstairs to the young girl selling hot water. I gave her a few copper coins and Peter asked about Lo. She looked frightened but exchanged several sentences with Peter. He pulled me aside.

"She says some Wa came and took Lo away. He had a bloody face but could walk. 'Wa' is a derogatory term for Japanese. It means dwarf. Sounds like ronin to me. She can't say where they came from or where they were going, just that they looked mean and were half-dragging, half quickstepping Lo away."

"Ask her when this happened."

Another exchange and then Peter said, "Two days ago."

"Ask her how she knows they were Japanese."

"She says they didn't speak Chinese. They spoke Wa. She knows because Chinese is a pretty language with tones and Wa has no tones."

"Let's get out of here. Do you have any idea where we are or how to get back to Frenchtown?"

Peter had another exchange with the young girl and give her some more copper coins. "She says Pan Lai Road is just down the next alley. That will take us to Chung Wha Road and Frenchtown."

"Let's get the hell out of here."

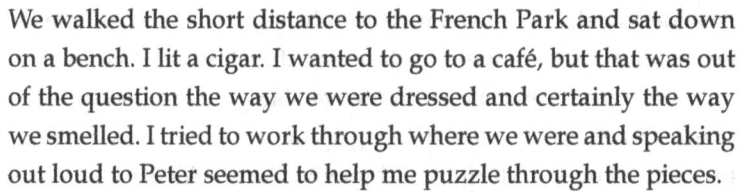

———∞———

We walked the short distance to the French Park and sat down on a bench. I lit a cigar. I wanted to go to a café, but that was out of the question the way we were dressed and certainly the way we smelled. I tried to work through where we were and speaking out loud to Peter seemed to help me puzzle through the pieces.

"Peter, I'm just trying to put it together, thinking out loud. Just listen, and then I'll listen. The Japs are definitely hunting Robin and that means Connie is in danger, too. I'm convinced that somehow all this is linked to their father and his activities in Central Asia. I can see the pieces but I can't fit them together. I want to increase security around Connie. Get Mikhail to recruit a couple more of his buddies. I want an around-the-clock watch on her, even when she and I are out together. I'll talk to Alan at Astor House and alert him to the threat, and I'll check in with the security head at the Cathay, too. I want you to check with the morgues and see if they have collected Lo."

I could see the look in his eyes. "I know, I know, it is probably fruitless. Do you know what Lo looks like?"

Peter shook his head no.

"Well, he's probably missing some teeth and is battered. See what you can discover. I don't want to miss a chance if he is still alive. We have so little to go on. I'd like to know what he knows and what he told the Japs. Okay, what am I missing?"

Peter looked at me and said, "If they are hunting Robin and Connie, then we are prey too."

"Yeah, you're right. Go armed whenever you can. I'll do the same. Ask your father to mobilize the other servants in our building and to be on the alert for any Japanese or anyone else who seems to be casing the building. I'll see you tomorrow."

Peter left and I just sat there thinking about next steps. I ticked them off in my mind in no order except the first one. First, call Connie and arrange to see her for breakfast. Give her an update. I needed to decide how much to tell her. I wanted to frighten her enough that she would follow my directions and be careful, but not so much that she would leave Shanghai or do something stupid. I needed to get a better grip on what the Japs were up to, so a call on the Marines and maybe Carroll Alcott. Get to the skeet club and find out who moved in Robin's circle and track them down. Get smarter on those Central Asia expeditions. Need to peel that onion. My two mysteries were one.

I felt myself getting angry. No place seemed safe, not even the Concessions. I got up to leave and found myself looking over my shoulder without even thinking, which only made me madder.

It was starting to get dark. Time to go home, hear "he lo he lo he lo," get a drink, and a bath. Especially a drink, maybe with the bath. I walked the few blocks to the Blackstone.

CHAPTER SEVEN
Wednesday-Thursday, January 13-14

Mikhail greeted me quietly as I walked into the lobby of the Cathay Hotel early the next morning. "All quiet, boss. I have added three more men: Josef, his brother Adrian, and a fellow I knew from my days in the White Army, Leonid. All solid. All good with a gun or a fist. I have set up a duty rotation. She will be covered around the clock."

"Thank you, Mikhail. I'm off to see the security head here, and then Miss Baker-Kerr and I will go to breakfast. Peter will drive us. I thought I'd take her to the Del Monte."

A big smile split his mustached face. "That will be a bit of an education, I think, for an English lady. I'll have Leonid there ahead of you. I'm going off now. I was the night man last night."

I nodded, smiled myself, and went to find the head of security for the hotel. Like security in most of the better places, it was a retired cop or soldier, this time from the British Indian army. Many of the doormen, the security guards for the more expensive stores, and all the traffic cops in the International Settlement were tall, very big Sikhs. An Indian army background helped to manage this proud and occasionally short-tempered workforce.

CITY OF LOST SOULS

Malcolm Iverson was Lt Col Iverson, British Indian Army (Rtd), as he liked to remind people.

I thanked Malcom for seeing me so early in the morning and filled him in on the threat. I told him my client was staying here and I had reason to believe she might be targeted by the Japanese or their agents. I told him I knew he and his staff were alert to all possible threats, but as a professional courtesy, I wanted to make him aware of this one. I told him about Mikhail and his team.

"They are professional, Malcom, and very discreet. I doubt your guests will notice them, but I am sure your men and the hotel staff would. I'd appreciate it if you consider them as just furniture for a few days."

"Furniture with guns, Jack?"

"That is for the street. They will not interfere or intervene in anything you do."

"I know they will not, because if they as much as get in the way of a boy emptying ashtrays, they will be on the street. Is that clear?"

"Of course, Malcom. I wouldn't want it any other way. Like I said, I am here as a professional courtesy. My men are here to accompany my client when she goes out. That is all."

I rang Connie in her room, and she joined me in the lobby. "I must say, Jack, 6:30 a.m. is an ungodly hour to be taking a lady to breakfast."

"I'm taking you to the Del Monte. It serves the best breakfast in Shanghai and is a must stop for any Shanghailander or visitor. Peter will drive us. It's on Avenue Haig in Frenchtown."

Avenue Haig was on the western end of the French Concession and had a reputation for sin. There were casinos and brothels but also some very nice apartment complexes. Like the Venus Club, the Del Monte was a late-night spot, someplace to go when other places started to slow down. It really didn't start hopping until

3:00 or 4:00 a.m. It had a floor show and taxi dancers of every description and nationality. It also served the best breakfast in Shanghai, according to us locals, starting at about 6:00 a.m.

"Jack, this looks like a night club," Connie said as we pulled up and I helped her out of the car.

"It is, but it also serves a great breakfast. Remember all those revelers we left last Saturday? Well, they end their night here or at the Venus Café in Hongkew. Or face down on the floor, I suppose. You're not a drunkard in Shanghai unless you drink at breakfast."

We walked in and sure enough there were about two dozen denizens of Shanghai in various states of evening dress, or undress in some cases, leaning over tables sipping coffee and trying to negotiate a large plate of scrambled eggs and bacon. We took a table a bit away from the others. I ordered the Del Monte special breakfast for the both of us.

"You are East of Suez, Connie, and like your Mr Kipling says, it's where the best is like the worst and there ain't no ten commandments and a man can raise a thirst. This place is operated by a couple of semi-shady characters, Al Israel and his brother-in-law Demon Hyde. Demon played some minor league baseball in California, and he plays for the local team here."

"Semi-shady?" she asked. "Shady comes in degrees then?"

"Oh yes. Shanghai has earned the reputation it has. Semi-shady because they operate the place but may not own it, and you can get an honest drink here, not worry about getting rolled, and they feed you a good breakfast and pour you into a car or rickshaw at the end of it."

I took a breath and leaned inward toward her. "Connie, I brought you here so you could get out of the hotel and see some of the local color. But I also need to talk seriously, and I did not want to do it in the hotel where others might hear us. I'm going to say it straight out. I think Robin is in danger and possibly you are, too. The Japanese are hunting him. And as of two days ago, they had not found him."

I could see worry in her eyes. "I don't know if they have found him. And I don't know why they want to find him, but I suspect it has something to do with your father and his work in Central Asia. Peter located Robin's Number One boy. When we went to speak to him, he wasn't there, and a local girl told us Japanese men had taken him away." I had decided not to tell her about the blood and the teeth. "Peter is continuing to look for the boy. Connie, is there anything that you can think of that would explain this?"

"Honest, Jack, I can't. As far as I know, father never had any dealing with Japan or the Japanese. He was just a scholar doing research on something he loved."

I looked into those blue eyes, and I believed her. "Well, I'm going to get to the bottom of this, and we will find Robin. But I'm also concerned about you. I have added some men, three more. Mikhail is in charge of protecting you. That athletic looking young man sitting near the bar is one of them. His name is Leonid. When you go out, they will be with you, but at a distance. Call it a defensive perimeter."

"Is this really necessary?"

"Yes. You're my client and you need to let me run this investigation, which now means protecting you as well as finding Robin."

"I have an appointment to see Mr Chu at the Oriental Library on Thursday next week. I want to be sure my father's papers arrived in good shape, and I want to talk to Mr Chu about hiring someone to help me finish putting them in order and preparing them for publication."

"Connie, I don't think you should cross Soochow Creek. The

Japanese have too much muscle in Hongkew and Yangtszepoo. Why don't you ask Mr Chu to meet you at the Royal Asiatic Society? Their offices are on Museum Road not far from mine. You can venture to the Oriental Library and inspect the papers when things settle down a bit. I'm sure Mr Chu is taking excellent care of them."

I got reluctant agreement from Connie, but also an immediate demonstration of independence.

"I've been invited to a party Sir Victor Sassoon is giving on Saturday. I'm going as a guest of the Crows, and since the party is in the Cathay Hotel, I should be safe." She paused, "But, I suppose I could use an escort, one with dinner clothes. Do you know anyone?" and she smiled.

"I have dinner clothes."

"Then it's settled. You may escort me." She took a bite of her breakfast "Say, these eggs are good."

We finished breakfast with small talk, but I could feel the tension. I wanted to ask her if she knew how to use a handgun and give her a small one for her handbag. But that would only increase the tension and wouldn't do her much good in a confrontation anyway. Might do just the opposite if she tried to use it. I told myself that Mikhail's team was the best protection, and I dropped the idea.

As the car pulled away, I asked her how she liked "Shanghai's best breakfast"

"It certainly was an experience. Not the sort of thing you'd see in Merrie Olde, but we are East of Suez. Do you Shanghailanders carry on like that every night?"

"Not all of us. I'm going to have Peter drop you off at the hotel, and then I'm going to start making some rounds and see if I can't pick up Robin's trail. A good friend of mine said he saw your father at the Shanghai Municipal Police Headquarters once.

Any idea of what that may have been about?"

"No. I was a small girl in England, and I doubt he would have said anything in my presence anyway. Might it just be something innocent?"

"It probably is. Just pulling at the loose threads. Ah, here we are at the Cathay. I'll check with you later. What are your plans for the day?"

"Mrs Crow and I are going to play tennis at the Recreation Grounds and then lunch."

"Enjoy your day." I could see Leonid on the sidewalk and Josef by the entrance.

I took a rickshaw to the Shanghai Rifle Club, which was in the building that housed the Portuguese social club. Every nationality in Shanghai had its own national association, national day celebration, and social club. Club Lusitano was the Portuguese one, and it was only a few doors down Yuen Ming Yuen Road from my office in the Missions Building.

It proved to be a fruitless effort on my part. The concierge told me Mr Robert Baker-Kerr had visited the club a time or two as a guest but that he was not a member. When I asked who he was the guest of, the concierge told me politely, but firmly, that the Shanghai Rifle Club did not share information about its members, especially with non-members. I thanked him and left making a mental note to drive out to the rifle range in Hongkew Park tomorrow and see if I couldn't find someone who knew Robin and would talk.

Peter was waiting for me in the office when I got back. He had made the check of the morgues as I asked. He said the River Police had pulled several adult males out of the Whangpoo River in the last few days but there was no telling for certain if any of them were Lo. They did recover one badly beaten man with broken and missing teeth the day after Lo disappeared. He had been worked over methodically judging from the bruises and broken bones before being dumped in the water. The interesting thing was that he was pulled from the river north of where Soochow Creek enters. That was the area with the heaviest concentration of Japanese in the Concessions.

———∞∞———

On Thursday, I decided to follow up on Father Jacquinot's sighting of Sydney Baker-Kerr at the Shanghai Municipal Police building. The headquarters of the SMP was on Foochow Road next to the Shanghai Municipal Council Building. The political section and Special Branch were on the upper floors. My relations with the SMP were about what you would expect if you read Dashiell Hammett, icy at best. I didn't think I would learn much, especially if Sydney had been working with the political or Special Branch boys, but I needed to at least try.

I had one contact in Special Branch who was slightly friendlier to me than his colleagues. He was a rare thing in the SMP, an American, but he was Irish, so I guess that gave him a cultural link to the rest of the force and made him acceptable. I asked the desk sergeant if Michael Finley was in and if so, would he tell him that Jack Ford would like to speak to him for a few minutes.

"He wants to know what it is about," the sergeant said to me putting his hand over the mouthpiece of the phone.

"Tell him I have some information that may be of interest to him about the Japs who have been causing trouble. Tell him if he comes down, I'll buy him a cup of decent coffee at the Metropole."

The Metropole was a few doors down from SMP headquarters and we quickly found a quiet table. Finley looked at me and said, "Well, Jack, do you really have something for us or are you just fishing for information you know you can't have?" Like I said, friendlier than the others, but that scale didn't extend all the way to friendly. Wary was the best you could get.

"I have some information that should interest you, but I'm also looking for some." I could see him lean back in his chair and start to get up. "Wait, Mike. Hear me out." I ran through what had happened at breakneck speed: Robin's disappearance, the search of his flat, the Japanese interest in both Robin and Connie, and the kidnapping and possible murder of the Number One boy.

Mike had a "so?" look in his eye but he was too polite to say it.

I said, "I think all this is connected to the work Sydney Baker-Kerr was doing in Central Asia, and he had some type of relationship with the SMP and Special Branch, in particular. So, fill me in, please. It will probably save one life and possibly two, if the brother is still alive." I was laying it on thick and stating as fact only what I suspected, but I had Mike's attention and interest.

"Jack, I'd like to help if I could, I really would, but I don't have the type of information you are asking for. At Special Branch, we worry about the security of the Concession, what the commies are doing, what the nationalists are doing, and what the Green Gang is doing mostly. I don't know what relationship this Baker-Kerr had with the SMP or even if he had one. It was long before my time on the force. If you want the Great Game stuff, you need to talk to Brit intelligence."

"Can you introduce me, Mike, or at least give me a name?"

"Listen to what I'm telling you. I don't know. You need someone who moves in those kinds of circles. A mick from Boston does not. I'll ask around a bit and see if anyone knows this Robert Robin fellow, and I'll get word to you one way or the other. But it's the best I can do. In return," he drew out in return and repeated it, "in return, I want you to tell me, in real time,

Jack, what you learn about the Japs. This place is about to go up like Guy Fawkes Night, I'm afraid."

I decided to press my luck. "I will Mike. I promise. Could you do one other thing for me?" I could see his eyes start to roll up, so I spoke quickly. "Mike, I don't think my client, Miss Baker-Kerr, is being entirely straight with me. Can you check around, nothing official, just see if anyone has heard of her?"

"Jack, this is a free port. Anyone can come here. Just buy a ticket and get off the boat."

"But Special Branch keeps an eye on who comes and goes. The Japs are definitely targeting her, and her father was a respected scholar who still has many friends here. And you just said, this city could explode at any time. Please, just ask around a bit and see what you can learn. That's all I'm asking. And it's the smart play. Get ahead of the situation rather than deal with the mess after. If something happens to her, her father's friends will raise hell and ask for heads. I'll buy you dinner at the Metropole."

He sighed. "Okay, Jack, I'll ask around the department and see if anyone knows anything about her. But you keep me informed on what you learn about Jap intentions, and I'm going to hold you to that dinner promise, even if I don't learn anything about her. Got it?"

I said I did, thanked him, promised him I would pass on anything I learned, signed the chit for the coffee, and sat there thinking about my next move.

———〜〜〜———

I moved down Foochow Road and stopped for some Shanghai noodles at the Summer Palace Restaurant. The day was half over. The municipal rifle range in Hongkew Park was one place to start but it was out of the way and would have to wait. I decided I needed to get a better understanding of what the Japanese might be up to and what the International Settlement was doing, if anything, about it.

Carroll Alcott was a news editor for the *Shanghai Evening Post and Mercury* and was one of the best-informed people on the Japanese. Along with John Powell of the *China Weekly Review*, Alcott was outspoken in support of the Nationalists and was continually reminding his readers of Tokyo's actions in Manchuria and North China. *The Post and Mercury* was only a few blocks away on Avenue Edward VII and I walked there as quickly as I could. The wind was picking up and it was cold.

Alcott had a stern visage that belied his good heart. With dark hair and bulky build, he looked every bit the tough reporter he was. And there was nothing soft about him, certainly not his attitude. He was already a thorn in the side of the Japanese militarists, and he added the German and Italian fascists before he left Shanghai. All three tried to kill or kidnap him at one time or another, and he was in the habit of carrying a .45.

I found him at the city desk chewing out some reporter. He looked up when he saw me walking toward him.

"Hi Jack. What brings you to this miserable excuse for a paper?" He turned back to the reporter. "I've seen more riveting copy in the Casper Wyoming Feed and Hay. Go fix it."

I wondered if there really were a Casper Feed and Hay but thought better of asking. "Got time for a beer, Carroll? I want to talk to you about the Japs and what they are up to."

"Yeah, sure," said with a mixture of frustration and anger in his voice. "There isn't going to be anything worth reading here for another couple of hours. Let's go to the Scandinavian Club down the street. The Danes make good beer."

We found a small table near the back and ordered a couple of Tuborgs. "Carroll, I may have a story for you, but this has to be off the record for now."

"I could use a good story. That paper is driving me crazy. I think I may leave. Anyway, sure, off the record, until you say otherwise."

Like with Finley I ran him through the basics of the last few days, then told him that I had spoken to Mike at the SMP who promised to look into things. That was an exaggeration, of course, but I wanted Carroll's help and I figured it didn't hurt to hype the story a bit to pique his interest. Besides, I really believed the Japs were up to something.

"Do you have any idea what the Japs may be up to? Why they would be chasing a junior employee of no apparent importance and his sister who just got off the boat?"

Carroll took a deep draw on his beer, and I signaled the waiter for two more. "Not really, but I can tell you that they are up to something here. Their ronin are going hard at the Nationalists and anyone or anything that offends the delicate sensibilities of their dear, divine emperor. Japanese diplomats even paid a visit to my editor-in-chief Randall Gould to complain about our coverage of China events. To his credit, Randall stood his ground."

He took a sip of the new beer. "I know the Japanese have been all over western China and Central Asia for years. There was a Count Otani who did some exploring out there about the same time as Stein. I think the Brits had their suspicions about his real intentions. Otani was a wheel in Buddhism in Japan, if I remember correctly, so it may have been legitimate. Maybe this Sydney Baker-Kerr found something they want or saw something they didn't want him to see."

"Father Jacquinot suggested the same thing."

"It wouldn't necessarily explain the Japs' interest in this Robin and his sister, but then again there may be a connection. Are you sure it was Japanese who grabbed the Number One boy?"

"There is a witness who says it was, and they had roughed him up pretty good. I found blood and a couple of teeth in his bare room."

"Look, Jack, I think the Jap militarists are capable of just about anything, and after Manchuria and North China, they have the bit in their teeth. They want all of China, and they are not going to let anyone get in their way. I would not be surprised if they tried something here like they did in Manchuria."

"Thanks, Carroll. I'm already taking precautions, and I'll let you know what I discover."

"Jack, just an idea from an old reporter. Brit intelligence is your best bet of learning if this Sydney chap was doing something for King and Country in addition to furthering his knowledge of early Buddhist theology. Rumor has it that a Roger Hollis at the British American Tobacco Company may have some link to His Majesty's Secret Service. Father Jacquinot may have some insight too."

CHAPTER EIGHT
Friday, January 15

I took the Packard Roadster in the morning and drove west toward the Columbia Country Club although it was the long way around to Hongkew Park and the rifle range. I wanted to avoid the traffic and the beggars that a direct route through the Concessions would involve. Besides, I liked the western suburbs. The city had expanded beyond the original grant of the Chinese by building a network of roads that was called the Extra Roads Area. This was Chinese territory, but the International Settlement ran it, in part because China was in such a state of disarray but mostly because the local Chinese preferred it that way. Victor Sassoon and a number of other taipans had large estates in the Extra Roads, and there were communities of single-family residences as well.

    I bore right onto Amherst Avenue, which was straight and lovely, shaded in the summer. It was favored by ex-pat professionals below the taipan level. The land was flat and open beyond the housing area with fields of vegetables and old burial mounds. The Shanghai Paper Hunt Club ran its version of riding to hounds in this area, a sort of point-to-point race chasing papers laid out in advance. The winner got to wear a red hunting coat. A bit of jolly olde England, unless of course it was your pitiful vegetable patch they were racing over.

I turned onto Keswick Road and headed north toward Jessfield Park and St. John's University, two gems of Shanghai. They were apart from, but still near to, all the sin and violence of the city. They were islands where Chinese and non-Chinese mixed, and in the case of St. John's, some of China's best young minds were educated. With its red and gray bricks, pagoda-style tiled roof, and vine-covered chapel, St. John's blended East and West in the best way.

Jessfield Park was the largest and for my money, prettiest of Shanghai's parks. It had a small zoo, and was open to Chinese as well as ex-pats. In the summer, the Shanghai Municipal Orchestra gave concerts, and there was a small lake on which children sailed toy boats while their parents and amahs watched from benches. There was a lovely teahouse, of course, and for those who required something stronger, there was Jock's Bar, a favorite hangout for members of the press and British enlisted men.

I turned right on Chung San Road and crossed Soochow Creek. In a few minutes I was parking near the rifle range, which was along one side of Hongkew Park. I had my new Browning 12-gauge with me, and the photo of Robin that Connie had given me. I went to find the range manager. He turned out to be a stuffy Brit in his late-40s or so. He had a military manner, an honest-to-God tweed jacket with leather patches, and a briar pipe.

I asked to use the range and spent about twenty minutes firing the shotgun. I could see him watching me, and I thought this might be my opening to start a conversation.

"Brand new. Just breaking it in and getting the feel of it," I said. "Never owned a semi-automatic before."

He took the bait. "Is that the Auto-5? Mind if I take a look at it?" I handed him the gun. "Type 3," he said, looking at the engraving along the side. "I always preferred the dog and bird scene." He hefted it to his shoulder, the barrel down range. I told him to go ahead and fire a few rounds, which he promptly did. "I am partial to the Browning myself," he said. "Always fine gunsmithing and it'll put the fear of God in any man."

I introduced myself and told him that I was hoping to run into a friend of a friend of mine here, but I didn't see him. "Maybe he was here earlier. His name is Robert Baker-Kerr. Perhaps you know him."

"I don't know the name, but he may have used the range. We get a great number of casual shooters like yourself, plus the regulars from the gun and rifle clubs."

I pulled the picture of Robin and Connie from my pocket and showed it to him. "Who's the woman?" he asked. I could see that he was getting suspicious.

"That is my lady friend and Robert is her brother. I was going to meet him for the first time here today." I could see that he wasn't entirely buying it.

"I've seen him here, but he isn't a regular."

I could see that this was going to go nowhere, and I decided to change tactics.

"Mister...Mister?"

"My name is Winningham."

"Mr Winningham, the young woman in the picture is Mr Baker-Kerr's sister and she is very worried about him. She has not seen him in several days and she asked me to look for him. She thought he might be here. I apologize for the small deception, but she is concerned and wants to keep his absence private." It was weak but at least Winningham didn't walk away.

"You said Baker-Kerr occasionally came here. He hasn't been

at his residence for some time. Do you know of anyone who might have some idea where he might be? Did he come here with a group of friends?"

A look of disgust came across Winningham's face. "I saw him here with that Donald MacBain."

"I don't know the name. Can you tell me where I might find him?"

"Butterfield and Swire, if they haven't sacked him. Some young men go to seed when they come East. MacBain looks like one of them to me, a carouser type who's fond of the grape and who knows what else. He came out to the range with a hip flask once, and I ran him off and told him never to come back. I tell you, MacBain is the kind of man that makes it harder for white men to hold things in check here, what with John Chinaman and the sons of Nippon running amok."

He started to walk away, and I asked, "What does MacBain look like? Any idea where he lives."

"Average height and weight but going to sod. A fruity little mustache you'd find on a frog or dago. I have no idea where he lives and do not care to know."

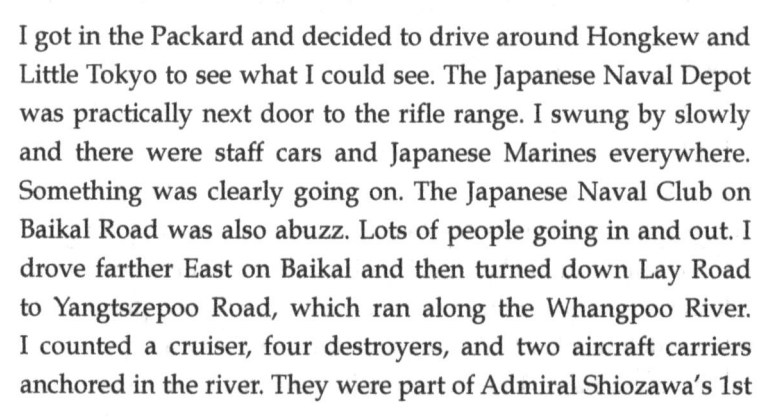

―――∽∞∽―――

I got in the Packard and decided to drive around Hongkew and Little Tokyo to see what I could see. The Japanese Naval Depot was practically next door to the rifle range. I swung by slowly and there were staff cars and Japanese Marines everywhere. Something was clearly going on. The Japanese Naval Club on Baikal Road was also abuzz. Lots of people going in and out. I drove farther East on Baikal and then turned down Lay Road to Yangtszepoo Road, which ran along the Whangpoo River. I counted a cruiser, four destroyers, and two aircraft carriers anchored in the river. They were part of Admiral Shiozawa's 1st

China Expeditionary Force. I hit Broadway and took the Garden Bridge across Soochow Creek and out of Hongkew.

Peter was at the office. I told him about my conversation with Winningham and what I had seen in Hongkew.

"We have a lead of sorts on Robin," I said. "We need to hunt down this Donald MacBain. I'll call Butterfield and Swire, but MacBain supposedly likes Shanghai's night life, especially the more risqué end of it. I want you to start scouting some of the sleazier Chinese clubs and see if they have heard of him. Also, check at the Villa Apartments and see if any of the servants remember him. They may even know where he lives."

Peter asked what he looked like, and I told him what I got at the range, average all around with a thin mustache. Peter left and I made three quick phone calls. The first was to Butterfield and Swire where I got the same brush off Connie and I had gotten at Jardine Matheson. MacBain was not in and that's all they would say. They did take my number and a request to have him call me.

The second call was to Finley at the SMP. I told him what I had seen in Hongkew. He thanked me for the update and asked if I had any luck finding Robin. I told him no, but that a Donald MacBain apparently was an associate of Baker-Kerr and might know something. I asked Finley if he knew him or knew of him. No to both, but he promised to ask around since I had honored my promise to keep him informed about what I saw the Japanese doing. He also said he was still asking around about Connie. I thanked him.

"You still owe me dinner, Jack."

My third call was to Captain Phil Bowman, the head of Regimental Intelligence for the US 4th Marines. I asked him to join me for a drink at Ma Jackson's Tavern on Bubbling Well Road, which was not far from Regimental Headquarters. I told him I had been over in Hongkew and Yangtszepoo and I wanted to tell him what I saw.

We sat at a table in the back of the bar. I filled him in on my actions and then asked what he was hearing.

"Well Jack, just what you are hearing and seeing. Things are very tense. We even have some Marines in defensive positions along Soochow Creek opposite Chapei. Admiral Shiozawa seems to be running back and forth between the Naval Depot and his flagship. Something's up, and there is a particularly nasty piece of work out and about stirring up trouble, a Major Tanaka of the Japanese Special Services. I think he has been behind some of the ronin activity."

"What do you know about a Tachibana who is probably military but doesn't advertise it?"

"Yeah, that's another one we try to keep an eye on. He is with the Japanese Consulate but it's not clear what his precise role is. He seems to be out and about town a lot, chatting up Shanghai's better classes. Very smooth. Could be intelligence, but like I said, we don't know."

"Any connection to this Tanaka?"

"Not that we know of. He may be involved but he's the type who would leave any dirty work to others."

I told him about Connie and Robin. "Any idea why a Japanese diplomat or intelligence officer would be interested in the Baker-Kerrs? There is a connection somewhere, but it is not clear to me."

"No, I have no idea. But if there is an intelligence angle, there is one person who may know, Roger Hollis with the British American Tobacco Company. It's an open secret that he is connected to the British secret services."

I asked what the 19th Route Army was doing. Phil shrugged his shoulders and said, "We know they are north and west of the city, but that's about all."

I stared at him for a second and shook my head. "You know, Phil, for an intelligence officer, you know damn little."

"Jack, intel is an imperfect art, not an exact science." We both laughed a little. I wasn't doing any better than Phil in uncovering secrets.

I paid for the beers, and we promised to stay in touch.

CHAPTER NINE
Saturday and Sunday, January 16-17

We met for cocktails in the Horse and Hounds Bar off the lobby of the Cathay Hotel, an hour before Sassoon's party. I thought I looked very elegant in my tailored dinner jacket and scarlet pocket square, but Connie looked ravishing. She had had her auburn hair done and it framed her face setting off those deep blue eyes. Her arms were bare and the light green dress — that color again — had a deep crescent-shaped neckline. The dress pinched in a bit just below the bodice, accentuating the effect, if that was possible. I just stared for a moment.

"Come now, Jack, it is not like you've never seen an evening gown before. Or what it might contain." I was trying to keep my eyes on her eyes, but they kept drifting down. She laughed softly and said, "My mother was quite attractive, and she told me, 'Constance, if God was good enough to be generous with you, then be good enough to share a bit of it...within reason.'" She laughed more deeply. "I do seem to have caught you off-guard."

"Sir Victor is going to love you," I said. We took a small table and ordered our drinks.

"What do you know about Sassoon?" I asked.

"Not much. He's the host and he is obviously very rich."

"Sir Victor's family are Baghdadi Jews who came here from India before the turn of the century. They made their money in the opium trade, and Sir Victor made millions more in real estate. He owns a lot of property in Shanghai and has been one of the people fueling the real estate boom here over the last decade. You are right about him being rich. He may be the richest man in Asia. It's either him or the Kadoorie family. "

Connie sipped her drink. "So, what's he like personally?"

"I can't say I know him. I don't even have a nodding acquaintance. I wouldn't be here tonight if I weren't your escort and if the Crows had not invited you to come as part of their party." I paused and took a pull on my martini. "I only know what others say. He's rich, but being a Jew makes him less than totally acceptable company for many of the Brits here. Oh, they'll drink his booze and attend his parties and do business with him, but in their eyes he's still the Jew who fled Bombay to avoid British taxes. I heard a taipan say once that Sassoon is an agreeable fellow but really a Philistine. I had to look up Philistine."

The Crows arrived and joined us. I explained Connie was asking about our host's background, and Carl leaped right in. "He's a bit of ladies' man, Connie, or at least he likes to think of himself that way. I dare say he will be struck by you. He may even ask you to pose for him, in fact. He is quite the amateur photographer. But don't do it. The word is that ladies and their garments can become separated when he starts snapping pictures."

Carl chuckled a bit and I had an idea of what was going through his mind, if only because I could see where his eyes were.

"He's rather good looking, in his early 40s, quite the

sportsman, and certainly well educated. Took his degree at Trinity College, Cambridge. A bit of a war hero, too. Was part of the Royal Flying Corps in the war. His plane crashed and he has a gimpy leg as a result. A bit of an outsider despite his wealth, being a Sephardic Jew."

Carl sipped his drink and continued. "He's a Baronet, you know. And he has his ways of reminding his British betters who is really in charge." Carl chuckled a bit and then said, "He likes these lavish parties, see. I'm sure we are in for a treat tonight. He especially likes costume parties. He once gave one with a circus theme. The guests had to dress as performers or animals. They all arrive and are enjoying the food and drink when Sassoon makes a grand entrance dressed as a ring master, whip and all, as if to say, 'I'm in charge of this circus and you'll dance to my tune.'"

Carl shook his head and laughed. "I really liked that one. He seems to tolerate Americans better than Brits."

It was a bit after 9:00 p.m. We finished our drinks and headed upstairs clutching our engraved invitations. The ballroom was on the eighth floor. There were twin marble staircases leading to the mezzanine where we caught the elevator to the upper floors. I had been in Shanghai for many years at this point, rubbed elbows with most of the famous and more notorious denizens of Shanghailand, and thought I had seen it all, but nothing like this.

The ballroom was very large, taking up most of the floor. There were gorgeous chandeliers over the sprung dance floor. Tables lined the room and there was a large bar with every imaginable liquor along one part of the wall. It was all art deco with indirect lighting, Lalique glass, and ten 'Ladies of the Fountain' set in niches above the wainscoting. Everything was either gold, silver, rose, or mother of pearl. The hotel orchestra led by Henry Nathan played the latest popular tunes. And if that wasn't enough, it was air conditioned, a very rare thing in those days.

Connie was as impressed as I was. "This is something you would see at Versailles." There must have been 250 people in the room, and it didn't feel crowded. The men were in white or black dinner jackets, and the women in their finest jewelry, which was as much on display as the ladies' flesh. Chinese waiters in black pants, white jackets, and soft slippers maneuvered in and out of the throng with trays of champagne, caviar, Chinese delicacies, cigars, and special orders. If it could be had in China, Sassoon had it and it was all here.

We had just found a table along the dance floor when a voice from behind me said, "I say, Carl, aren't you going to introduce me to this lovely lady?" I turned and it was Sir Victor. He was very elegant in a dark dinner jacket with a carnation in his lapel. He was leaning a bit on a walking stick with a carved ivory head, and there was a monocle in his right eye. A silver cigarette holder was in his right hand.

"Ah, Eve, of course. Miss Baker-Kerr please meet Sir Ellice Victor Elias Sassoon, our host. Eve, this is Miss Constance Baker-Kerr, a newcomer to our little town. She's staying here at the Cathay."

"A most welcome addition," he said, "I must say. Carl is a little too elaborate with the introduction. Most people call me Sir Victor, but my friends call me Eve, the initials, you know. I hope you'll be my friend. I trust you have found everything at the hotel to your liking. We try to provide exceptional service and comfort."

Perhaps Carl's warning was echoing in her head and perhaps not, but Connie said, "Then you must call me Connie, as all my friends do, and your hotel is...is...is...I can't quite find the right words to express it. 'Marvelous' does not do it justice."

"Well, perhaps we can have tea some afternoon. If there is anything you need, please just ask, and I'll do my humble best to provide it. It was nice meeting you. Enjoy the evening and we must have tea before you leave. Sigh, I must go greet my other guests now," and he bowed slightly and made his way around the room. That was the first of two surprise encounters that evening.

I took two flutes of champagne from a tray and handed one to Connie. "You seem to have made a new friend," I told her.

Music filled the room, competing with the cigar and cigarette smoke. Connie and I danced and danced. It was after midnight when a second surprise encounter occurred. We were once again on the dance floor when I felt a light tap on my shoulder. I turned and a tall Japanese gentlemen asked if he might cut in. I was taken aback a bit and he took advantage of the moment by grasping Connie's hand and leading her deeper onto the dance floor.

I went back to our table and sat down with the Crows. "Who is that?" I asked Carl.

"That is Zuicho Tachibana of the Japanese Consulate and I think an officer in the Imperial Navy." I sank into my chair, stunned.

It was several minutes before Mr Tachibana escorted Connie back to our table. He bowed deeply at the waist, thanked me for allowing him the great pleasure of dancing with Miss Baker-Kerr, and said he hoped to see her again some time. He turned and melded into the crowd.

"What did he say?" I asked Connie.

"It was all very cordial, very pleasant, except, of course, that I knew he had been hunting my brother and me. As we danced, he said he was familiar with my father's work and that he was a great admirer. He said it would be a great honor for him if we had the opportunity to have lunch and discuss it one day. He asked after my brother and said he hoped he was well. I didn't know what to say, so, I said he is. A bit more small talk and that's all. What in the hell was that all about, Jack?"

The Crows had been on the dance floor and were coming back. "Let's go out on the balcony where we can talk in private."

The balcony ran the length of the ballroom and overlooked The Bund. It was chilly and I draped my coat over Connie's shoulders.

I said, "I have no idea but I'm sure it wasn't accidental. Maybe he doesn't know that we know the Japanese are searching for Robin and he was fishing to see if you would say something."

I looked at the lights and the buildings on The Bund. The noise of the city was far, far away. The stars glittered and the only scent was Connie's perfume. I thought about the old Chinese woman who had spilled her meager noodles in the street. I could hear the music and the sounds of laughter and clinking champagne flutes from the inside. We were above all the hurt and pain and the daily struggle to eat. We didn't live in the same city. We didn't live in the same world.

I put my arm around Connie, and she leaned into me. I said, "I don't know what Tachibana is up to, but I'm sure it is not a desire for a pleasant conversation about your father's work."

"He frightened me, Jack, even as we were dancing. It was nothing he did or said, but I didn't like it. The way he talked. The way he implied he knew a lot about my father, Robin, and me."

I pulled her a bit closer and looked into her eyes. She closed them and I kissed her. She pressed hard against me and kissed me passionately. As she stepped back, I saw her wipe a tear from her eye.

"I'm here. You are not alone. I'll find Robin and deal with Tachibana and his gang if necessary."

I guided her back into the ballroom where we sat closer together, held hands under the table, and clung to one another when we danced. I was getting in deep. That moment on the balcony has stayed with me all these years.

———∞———

I slept late Sunday then dressed casually and went to see Father Jacquinot at Aurora. Services were over and I caught him before confessions started. He greeted me with that big smile and said, "Fu Fei, are you here to lighten that soul of yours?"

"I need help but not that kind," I replied. I filled him in on what I had seen in Chapei and Hongkew and the encounter with Tachibana.

"I think the Japs are up to something and I can't for the life of me figure out why they are so interested in Connie and her brother."

Ever the Jesuit, Jacquinot said, "The Japs are up to something alright, and this Tachibana is interested in the Baker-Kerrs, but the two are not necessarily causal, Jack. Related perhaps, but they can be independent. Tachibana's interest may be personal. See what I mean?"

"I get that," I said, "but that still leaves me with the why, Father. Mike Finley and Captain Bowman both think Roger Hollis may be able to help me, and they said you have an in with him. Is that the case? Can you broker a meeting? You know everyone, and as the Chaplain for the Shanghai Volunteer Corps, you move in the security circles. I want to ask him about Sydney Baker-Kerr."

"Yes, I know Hollis, and I'll see if he will meet with you. And yes, Mr Hollis of the British-American Tobacco Company has ties to the British security services. I know he is concerned as we all are about Japan and its intentions in China. You may interest him. I'll see and I'll call you tonight one way or the other."

"Another question, Father. Do you know a Donald MacBain?

He is an associate or friend of Robin. He works for Butterfield and Swire."

"I don't know him. MacBain? A Scotsman, I presume. If Mr MacBain is a bonnie highland laddie, you might look for him at the Church of St. Andrew on Broadway in Hongkew or the St. Andrew Society. He probably belongs to one of them if not both."

"I hadn't thought of that. That's a good idea." I paused. "What do you think will happen with the Japanese and the Chinese?"

"I'm very concerned. The Institute of the Holy Family Convent is on North Honan Road near the North Train Station. Seizing control of the station will be a major objective for both the Japanese and the Nationalists if fighting breaks out. It is a very heavily populated area, too, with many refugees."

I thanked him and told him I'd wait for his call. As I left the Aurora campus, I saw an elegant Chinese gentleman in a silk brocade gown with long sleeves and turned up cuffs, from which extended tattered woolen underwear. Shanghai.

Father Jacquinot called a little before 10:00 p.m. Hollis would see me at the Shanghai Club at 1:00 for tiffin.

CHAPTER TEN
Monday Morning, January 18

On the Monday, the fuse was lit. It was a day I will never forget.

The first indication I had was a call early Monday morning from Mike Finley at the Shanghai Municipal Police. "Jack, I have a bit of information for you on MacBain and on your client Baker-Kerr, but first have you heard about the attack on the Japanese monks? Do you know anything about that?"

What attack? was all I could think of to say. "It's not clear exactly what happened or why," Mike said, "but at least one monk is dead, and a number of others are hurt. The Japs are going crazy, raising holy hell. It happened at one of their factories, the…the…I've got it here someplace…the Sanyo Towel Factory in Chapei. There has been a lot of labor trouble with the Chinese workers there and it's Japanese-owned. The Japanese are talking about sending troops into the area to protect their property."

"Mike, that's Chinese territory. Is this Manchuria all over again?"

"I don't know, but it will get out of hand pretty quickly if we don't get on top of it. The 19th Route Army commander isn't going to sit by if he has his way. The Shanghai Municipal Council is trying to calm the Japanese and the mayor of Chinese Shanghai is trying to keep his Nationalist subjects in check."

I told him I had planned to look for MacBain in Hongkew this afternoon. "I have something for you on that but if you do go, will you call me after and tell me what you see? I think the SMC will be meeting and they will expect Special Branch to tell them what's going on."

"Of course. What about MacBain?"

"About eight months ago, a beat cop found him bleeding in an alley off Jukong Road. He had been rolled and robbed. He took him to the Lester Hospital. He had been drinking in some of the rougher joints near the trenches. This wasn't the first time he got in over his head, according to the guys I talked to. They suggest you cruise some of the bars in the Jukong area, Blood Alley, or the places that feature White Russian dancers. Your boy seems to like the less genteel side of our great metropolis. Not a lot to go on Jack, but somewhere to start. I hope it helps."

"It does Mike, but what about my client?"

"Well, this is just gossip mind you. Nothing I know for certain, but one of the officers here had friends on the same ship she was on. She apparently cut quite a figure on the way here. Low-cut gowns, flirting with the male passengers, married and unmarried. Upset the church ladies on board no end. They claim she had a shipboard romance with a British officer and that they were, to use their term, intimate. Could be just jealous old biddies, Jack.

"But there is something else, and it could be serious, and perhaps even related to your case somehow. She apparently left England under a cloud. It's unclear why. Something about a messy affair but also rumors — and that's all they are, according to my officer friend — that she was accused of stealing some artifacts or something. I queried Oxford and she is not wanted or even suspected of anything. So, it may be nothing."

"Thank you, Mike, for the lead on MacBain and the information about my client. I'll give you a call when I get back from Hongkew this afternoon and keep you posted on anything I might find out in the future."

I called Peter and filled him in on what Finley told me. I also told him to bring Connie to the office immediately, even if he had to drag out of the hotel by her hair.

Peter said he had been back to the Villa Apartments where he again talked to the servants. Several of them said a person who might be MacBain had visited Robin several times, but they did not know his name or where he lived. Peter said he looked around some of the brothels on Fukien Road but got nowhere, and then did a quick turn through some of the lower end nightclubs in Little Russia in Frenchtown that also turned up nothing. I asked Peter to check out the flats in the western section of the Concessions that Butterfield and Swire had for their junior employees.

Then I made ready to meet Connie at my office.

"Sit down. You lied to me."

"How have I lied to you?" flashing her temper. "How dare you speak to me in that tone!"

"I told you at the start that I play straight and I expect my clients to be straight with me. You haven't been. You haven't told me why you really left England or the kind of trouble you were in there."

"Trouble?"

"You use men and you are trying to use me. I'm not going to let that happen. Why did you leave England and why are you here? Were the police sniffing around? Is that stuff you shipped here really your father's?"

"Who have you been talking to? Where did you get these ideas?"

"Answer my questions now or I am dropping you and this case. You can deal with the Japs on your own and good luck finding your brother."

I moved toward the door to the outer office as if to open it. She had been half out of the chair but now sat back and took a breath. She took a cigarette from her bag and lit it with the gold lighter. She held it up where I could see it.

"Like it? It was a gift...from a lover. I am not a young, naïve girl, Jack. I have had affairs but I don't use men to get things. In fact, I have not had much luck with men, including the Oxford don I told you about. He was a bastard. He is one of the reasons I came here. I also came here because there was no one left for me in England. Partly because my brother was here. And partly to finish my father's work."

"Tell me about the don."

"You mean was he married and did I sleep with him? Yes, to both. But he was using me. He was jealous of my father's discoveries. He started to spread stories. I learned he told people that he didn't think my father's work was all his or that the artifacts were genuine. At the same time, he was copying from my father's journals and planning to publish first. I caught him trying to take one of the scrolls when he thought I was asleep. That was the end of the affair, and soon after he was spreading stories about me and my father's work among the faculty. A couple of his fellow dons even chatted me up to see if I might be 'available'.

"Not a pretty picture, Jack. So, I wrote his wife and included a snippet of his hair. We had another angry meeting and he threatened to go to the authorities and raise questions about the artifacts. It was a nasty, little academic catfight with a lot of hissing but with some sharp, little claws, too.

"I didn't lie to you. I just didn't tell you everything. In fact, it is really none of your business. I had a difficult relationship with my mother, but I adored my father, and I was not going to see his name smeared. So, I decided to come here, and I sent the artifacts on ahead so the don couldn't get his hands on them or come up with some pretext to have the police or the University impound them."

She took a long drag on the cigarette and snuffed it out on the corner of my desk.

"What about the Japanese?" I said.

"I told you I don't know any Japanese and I have no idea why they seem to be interested in me and my brother. I won't go back to England ever. I won't give up looking for my brother. And I won't stop until I see my father's work published and recognized. You know, maybe I'm not all that different from some of the women we saw in the dance halls. Just another coaster who washed up here looking to start over. That's what you are too, Jack. Someone who's stuck and can't go back or won't go back. We are more alike than you think. A couple of lost souls hiding out in a lost city." She stopped and looked me directly in my eyes. "So, Jack, are you going to help me find my brother?"

I walked across the room and sat down opposite her. I believed her. I took her hand, and said, "Yes."

CHAPTER ELEVEN
Monday Afternoon, January 18

The Shanghai Club at No. 3 The Bund was famous (or notorious) for three things: the Long Bar with its strict seating protocol; pink gin lunches; and a snobbishness that made London clubs seem democratic by comparison. Needless to say, I was not a member.

The concierge greeted me at the door and quickly turned me over to a white-coated house boy who led me upstairs to a small private dining room. I glanced in at the Long Bar as we walked past. By tradition, the river pilots sat nearest the windows where they could watch the harbor. The taipans all had reserved positions along the bar depending on the importance of their firm and their social standing. Jardine Matheson and Butterfield & Swire were well represented as was the Shanghai and Hongkong Bank and the other major financial and commercial enterprises. There were no women, no Chinese, and no Sassoons, Hardoons, or Kooderies because they were Jews.

Roger Hollis was waiting for me. "Welcome, Mr Ford. I have taken the liberty of ordering lunch for us. Please have a pink gin and tell me how I might be of assistance."

I took the gin and sat down opposite Hollis. His hairline

was starting to recede, but his dark bushy eyebrows seem to be growing as compensation. A wry, pleasant smile was set in an unremarkable face. I guess that is a good thing if you do secret work. I ran quickly through the basic facts for him.

"Mr Hollis, I believe Sydney Baker-Kerr had some sort of relationship with the British government, and that is the reason the Japanese are searching for his son Robert and why Mr Tachibana is interested in Miss Baker-Kerr. Can you shed any light? It may save a young man's life, and his sister's."

Hollis leaned back in his chair and took a sip of his drink. The waiter brought in lunch. It was a horrid mixed grill with some over boiled vegetables. There was also a bottle of wine. Hollis waited for the waiter to leave, clearly considering what, and undoubtedly how much, to say.

"Might we reach a bit of an understanding before we go any further?" I nodded. "Good, I agreed to this meeting because Father Jacquinot asked me to lunch with you. Are you Roman Catholic by any chance, Mr Ford?"

I told him I was raised in that Church. "Well good, then you'll understand when I tell you that anything that is said in this room is said as if it were in the Confessional of your church. Am I clear?"

"Yes. Nothing said here is to be repeated."

"Precisely." He took a sip of wine and moved a portion of the mixed grill onto the back of his fork, glanced suspiciously at it, and then put it in his mouth. "Must do something about the chef. Anyway, His Majesty's Government's interests are far-flung, but its resources are more limited. So, at times we ask citizens who may be able to do so to lend a hand by...mmm...being observant and sharing their observations."

His round-about conversation was beginning to grate but there was nothing to be done. I wanted to leap in and speed up things but resisted. He had information and he seemed willing to share some of it, but under his conditions and at his pace.

"Sydney Baker-Kerr was one of those. As you know, Great Britain has long worried about Russian expansion in Central Asia and toward India. After the Czar's defeat in 1905 by the Japanese, we began to monitor Tokyo's activities as well. Count Otani financed three expeditions to Central Asia in the same area where Sir Aurel Stein was also active. On one of them were two men dressed as monks of the Pure Land Sect of Japanese Buddhism. One was named Nomura and the other Tachibana. We, that is His Majesty's Government and the India Office, were suspicious of the two, because we had information they were actually officers of the Imperial Army and Navy, respectively."

He had my full attention now. He took a sip of the wine and continued. "This claret is not bad. Anyway, they may have been two co-religionists pursuing an interest in classical Buddhist texts, but it also occurred to us they might also be scouting and mapping the territory against some future need. In as much as the Stein expedition was operating at the same time in the same area, Mr Baker-Kerr kindly agreed to keep his eyes and ears open and share any observations with our Consulate in Kashgar on his way home via Simla and India.

"Baker-Kerr made some interesting discoveries of his own, as you know. There was a falling out with Stein, however, and he left the expedition. When he arrived in Kashgar with his servant, a Chinese Muslim, he was suffering from a high fever. Before he died, he told our Consul General that he had observed the two Japanese with surveying and mapping equipment. They also saw him because they attacked his camp one night. Baker-Kerr and his servant were able to chase them off but not before Baker-Kerr took a bullet in the shoulder. It went septic on the journey to Kashgar and that was the source of the fever that killed him.

Now you know what I know. Care to join me in a Port?"

"I don't know what to say."

"About the Port?"

"No, and I'll take the glass of Port. I'm beginning to think I need it. Some of the pieces are coming together. I'm thinking out loud, but presumably Tachibana and Nomura attacked Baker-Kerr because they did not want their activities known. Baker-Kerr makes it to Kashgar with his knowledge and artifacts intact. Before he dies, he passes on what he knows to your Consul General and sends most of his discoveries home to England. But has his servant, Ding Mu, hold his most important finds until his son or daughter can claim them. Tachibana cannot be sure what Baker-Kerr passed on about what he had seen or what might be in the materials he sent home. So, when Robert arrives, he sees an opportunity to find out what Robert knows. The same for Constance. Only Robert has disappeared. That sound plausible?"

"Well, it makes as much sense as anything I can think of, but we really cannot know Tachibana's motive. He may be acting on his own or at the direction of Tokyo. In either case, it does not matter. They are clearly hunting the son, and I am inclined to agree that Miss Baker-Kerr is at risk as well. I've been of some assistance, then? Now perhaps you can help me a bit."

That did not come entirely as a surprise. I expected there would be a price for the information he had. "If I can, certainly."

"Splendid then. Do you know or have you heard of a Major Tanaka of the Japanese Special Services? He is quite a nasty little man. He was one of the engineers of the Mukden Incident, and we strongly suspect he staged yesterday's attack on the five Japanese Buddhist priests as a pretext for a move against the Chinese Nationalists."

"No, I do not know him. The name means nothing to me."

"I think it will in time. He has been active with the ronin. If anything were to befall Robert or Constance, he may well be the reason. As you go about your search, do keep an eye out for him and an ear open. We'd be very appreciative to learn whatever you learn."

"I promise. One last question if I may. Does the name Donald MacBain mean anything to you? He apparently is an acquaintance of Robert and may have some information about his whereabouts."

"I'm sorry I do not. But if I come across anything, I will pass it on."

"Thank you very much, Mr Hollis. This has been very helpful."

"Oh, Jack, please call me Roger now that we are working in tandem," he said with a small wink and that wry smile. "The food here is not all I might hope for, but the wines are quite good, don't you agree?"

I took a rickshaw across the Garden Bridge and into Hongkew. Broadway was one of the main drags of this section of the city and the Church of St. Andrew was near Astor House. The area was a busy one, but the church had a low stone wall and a lovely garden that gave it an air of peace. I walked around the back to the rectory. I found a deacon sweeping leaves off a brick path. I introduced myself and told him I was looking for Donald MacBain.

"A friend told me that he might be parishioner and you might know where I might find him," I said. I could tell by the sour expression on his face that he knew the name.

"May I ask why you want to see him? Are you with the police?" That was an odd response, I thought, but it told me that he knew MacBain and didn't think much of him.

"No, I am not with the police. Mr MacBain may have some information about the whereabouts of a relative of a friend of mine. I'm trying to help is all."

"Well, Mr MacBain is a parishioner, but we see very little of him, and frankly he would do his health and his soul considerable good if he spent more time here than on the town."

"Do you know where he lives or how I might reach him?"

"I believe he works for Butterfield and Swire and resides in one of their company flats. I don't know more, and if I may offer a bit of advice for the relative...Well, one's own reputation is enhanced or diminished by the company one keeps." And with that he turned and began to vigorously sweep the path. I got out of there.

The Japanese Special Services was a section of the dreaded Japanese Military Police, the Kempeitai. They had set up shop in the New Asia Hotel in Hongkew on the border with Chapei, and it was already getting a reputation as a place where Chinese went in and never came out, or if they did it was in the river. I wondered if that is what had happened to Lo. It was only a few blocks west of St. Andrew, and I took a rickshaw to see what I could see.

I had the puller drop me off down from the New Asia. It was unremarkable building that looked like it catered to Japanese and Chinese businessmen, but judging from the Japanese Blue Jackets out front, the Imperial Navy and the Kempeitai had taken it over. I stepped into the street and looked for a place where I could watch the building. The din hurt my ears and a stiff breeze from the west drove the smell of human waste, rotting vegetables, joss sticks, and heaven knows what onto my clothes and skin. My eyes watered and I resisted the desire to cover my face with my handkerchief.

There were some street stalls across from the New Asia and I walked down to one that sold sundries. It was just a sheet of wood on two Chinese sawhorses draped with a piece of cloth. On it was old hammer, a hacksaw blade with a couple of teeth missing, and assorted springs, screws, and bolts, all of which had been scavenged from somewhere. A small boy sat behind the makeshift counter repairing an umbrella that had seen much better days. There was an awning and when I stood under it, I could see the front and one side of the New Asia.

There were guards with rifles and fixed bayonets at the corners of the building and two Blue Jackets in starched uniforms by the front door. They snapped to attention and presented arms when Japanese, including some who were not in uniform, entered or left. I stood there for about twenty minutes and watched as cars, some with pennants and motorcycle outriders, dropped off their passengers. A few had what I took to be aides who carried dispatch boxes and map cases. This was no casual gathering.

I decided to walk up the road to where I could see around the back of the building. There was a parking area where there with a number of motorcycles, patrol cars, and a couple of large trucks with canvas sides. A group of rough-looking men, Chinese or Japanese I could not tell, were loading fuel cans into the trucks.

I was in plain sight, and one the Japanese guards noticed me watching the loading operation. He crossed the street and shouted at me in Japanese. Then, with his rifle at port arms, he shoved me in the chest I stepped back with the blow, and he did it again, a smile on his face. He had his finger in the trigger guard of the rifle, and when he started at me again, I stepped in, grabbed the rifle by the stock and by the barrel, and twisted it up and out. I heard his finger break. I could see a couple of his buddies heading my way. Time to leave and I walked briskly to

CITY OF LOST SOULS

the General Hospital a short way away and ducked inside.

I called both Finley and Hollis from my office and told them what I had seen. I did not mention my confrontation with the Japanese guard. I told them about the truck, the stream of important people, and the map cases. I asked Hollis if he had a picture of Major Tanaka, because if he did, I could drop by and see if Tanaka was one of the men I had seen. Hollis did not. We promised to keep one another informed.

Peter was back and he reported on his day. He had gone to the flats used by Butterfield and Swire's junior employees and found out that MacBain did live there, but often was away.

"MacBain's Number One boy clearly does not like his master, and I was able to bribe him with a few coppers to let me look around," Peter said. "The servant said he has not seen MacBain since Friday morning but that's not unusual. MacBain often disappears over the weekend and sometimes doesn't return until mid-week. There was nothing much in the flat that reflected MacBain, except for a very nice set of ivory opium pipes that looked used and an album of photos. I went through the album and lifted these two pictures."

The first was in color and showed a thin, young man with a little mustache and straw-colored hair. Next to him in the photo was Connie's red-headed brother, Robin. The second photo was a black and white head shot of dark-haired woman with a Garbo-shaped face and a cigarette in her full lips. Smoke wreathed her, and her right eye was squinting.

"This is great, Peter. The man next to Robin has to be MacBain. It matches the description I had from Winningham. Why did you take the picture of the woman?"

"There were a number of pictures of her in the album, some

with not a lot on. I figure she must be important to him. She looks Russian to me. Might be a taxi dancer or a prostitute."

"You're probably right. Anyway, it is a place to start. We have just the one picture of MacBain. I want you to take it and start showing it around some of the dens that cater to Westerners since he apparently likes opium, and to the salt-water sisters. See if anyone recognizes either MacBain or Robin. I'll take the other photo around the dance halls and see if I can't find this particular Sonya.

When you're looking for trouble in Shanghai, there are limitless opportunities. I wasn't going to exhaust all the possibilities in one night, especially after the day I had, so I decided to leave the brothels for the next day. As Peter started canvasing the 'flower smoke rooms' for western opium users, I decided to start at the top of the Russian taxi dancer places and work my way down. Connie and I had been to the Ambassador and the Black Cat a week ago, so I thought I'd start at the Casanova where I knew the manager, Tom King.

The Casanova was in the International Settlement on Avenue Edward VII. The Nanking Theater was across the street in the French Concession. This made the Casanova a handy place to be if you had to beat a hasty retreat from the Shanghai Municipal Police. Cross the street and you were in French territory. Of course, it worked both ways and although both police forces had the right of "hot pursuit," the antagonism between both impeded cooperation.

It was a top-tier nightclub with a huge ballroom and some of the prettiest Russian hostesses. Its clientele reflected the variety that was Shanghai. You could see wealthy Taipans out on the town, elegant Chinese gentlemen in very fine silk gowns, a variety of military uniforms, spouses, mistresses, movie stars, and ordinary people, too. And dozens of languages and dialects.

CITY OF LOST SOULS

The bar staff were true polyglots as long as you limited the conversation to your drink order.

I pulled one of the bar boys aside. "Massa King topside no topside?" I got a sharp shake of the head and a finger pointing to a corner of the room. Tom was there in his dinner jacket and red carnation talking to one of the swells. I weaved my way between tables, hostesses, and dancers.

"Hi Tom. Can I speak to you privately for a few minutes?"

"Sure, but let's get out of this racket. We can go to my office in the back."

I followed him to a corridor behind the bar and then upstairs to a small office.

"Still drinking Laphroaig?" he asked as he poured me one from his private stock.

"When I can't get a martini. How do you remember?"

"Ah, it's the secret to running a good establishment. That and some muscle when you need to handle the drunks. How can I help you?"

I pulled the picture from my pocket and handed it to him. "I'm working a case, Tom, and I'd like to find this girl. Do you recognize her? I think she is Russian and may be a taxi dancer."

"I don't recognize her, Jack, and I think you're wasting your time showing a picture around. There must be 7,000 White Russians in Shanghai. There are hundreds of taxi dancers, hookers, and thousands of average Sonyas. Can you tell me why you want to find her? I may be able to help."

"I'm working a missing person case. She is probably the girlfriend of the friend of the guy I'm looking for. Do the names Robert Baker-Kerr or Donald MacBain ring a bell? Baker-Kerr has red hair, in his twenties. He goes by Robin sometimes. He's the guy I'm looking for. MacBain is blondish, also in his twenties, and is going to seed according to some people I've talked to."

"That hardly narrows the field in this city, Jack, except for the red hair. Baker-Kerr, no, but I think we may have escorted MacBain out of here a couple of times. Let me check." He picked up the phone and dialed one number. "Paul, do we have a Donald MacBain on our list of problem guests?" He listened for a couple of minutes then nodded his head and said, "Thanks, Paul. Keep an eye out for him and let me know if he turns up."

"Paul watches the doors and keeps order. He says this MacBain isn't a troublemaker per se, but we've had to pour him into a taxi a time or two. He doesn't get loud or belligerent, according to Paul, just stumbles into paying customers. I'll keep an eye out and I'll give you a call if we see him."

"Thanks Tom."

I knew Tom was right that showing the picture around was probably a waste of my time, but I thought I'd try Del Monte's. It was only 1:30 a.m. and that place didn't get hopping for another couple of hours. It also had the most Russian taxi dancers in Shanghai. When Connie and I had had breakfast there, the girls were gone. Now would be a good time to give it a shot.

I took a taxi from the Casanova. I did not have an in with the management at Del Monte's, so I bought a couple of drinks, danced a few dances, and showed the picture to some of the girls. They did not recognize her or if they did, they were not saying. I spent an hour and then decided to step down several levels and made for The Frisco in Blood Alley.

Blood Alley, Rue Chu Pao San actually, was a short street off Avenue Eduard VII in the French Concession, and it had at least fifty bars on it. It was a hangout for all the world's navies. You could always get a steak, cheap beer, only slightly more expensive women, and a black eye all in the same night.

The places ranged from the appropriately named Chez Smell Bad to the better establishments, better being a relative term, like the Palais Cabaret, Mumm's, the Crystal, George's Bar, the New Ritz, and Monk's Brass Rail. A lot of the bars were owned or managed by men like Monk, who was an obese ex-sailor with a quick temper and a baseball bat beneath the bar. It's there to even the odds when the fighting starts, he once told me.

The Frisco and the Palais Cabaret were the cream of this particular crop, and the Frisco featured white women, many of whom were Russian. A lot of the places in Blood Alley were just bars, but some had Chinese prostitutes. They were mostly refugees from the countryside and in many cases, they had been sold to the bars by their parents. The Shanghai Municipal Council ran the Door of Hope, which rescued young girls and boys from brothels, but Blood Alley was on the French side of the street.

The beggars were out in force as always hoping for a dirty coin or a scrap of leftover food. They were mostly mothers in rags with naked children at their breast. All were suffering from malnutrition and some of the children had been maimed to make them more sympathetic as beggars. There was a beggars' guild of a sort that sometimes threatened to flood a merchant's doorway with the destitute unless a payment was made. The floods in Central China and the fighting between warlords had swelled the ranks of the desperate.

I did what I had done at Del Monte's, bought some drinks, chatted up the girls, and showed the picture around. And again, got nowhere. I left feeling dirty. As I took a rickshaw back to the Blackstone, I could see a red-orange glow and smoke in Chapei.

CHAPTER TWELVE
Tuesday, January 19

I slept late the next morning and then took Connie to lunch at Jimmy's Kitchen, a Shanghai institution, as was Jimmy James himself. Everyone agreed that he had been a US serviceman, but some said he had been in the army, others in the Marines, and the romantics claimed he was a sailor who had jumped ship in Shanghai. It didn't matter. He was quite the entrepreneur. His restaurant had a couple of locations, plus he owned the Handy Bar and the St George's Cabaret in Frenchtown.

We went to the Jimmy's Kitchen on Nanking Road not far from the Cathay and the Missions Building. The place was always dark, and the menu was huge. It came in a binder and ran to a number of pages. There were always pickled onions, ketchup, and blue enamel salt and pepper shakers on each table and some slot machines by the bar. Jimmy served American food and the portions were large. Leftovers went into paper bags that the customers or Jimmy's staff handed out to the beggars behind the restaurant. Jimmy was a tough guy with a tender heart.

I filled Connie in on what I had learned but spared her the details of her father's death or his assistance to the British

Government. I did tell her that Tachibana and a man named Nomura had been part of an Otani expedition, and they had probably encountered her father at some point. I told her there were suspicions that Tachibana and Noruma were really intelligence officers, and I speculated her father may have seen something and reported it to the British Consul General in Kashgar.

"If Tachibana believes that, then it might explain why he is so intent on finding your brother and talking to you, to see if you know something," I said.

"There is nothing in my father's papers about Otani or meeting any Japanese. It's all about the movement of Buddhist thought to China."

"What about the materials he left with his servant?"

"All we have is a general description from the letter that was in with the artifacts he shipped home. It just said that he had uncovered some fascinating material on the origins of the Kaifeng Jews and perhaps even a piece of the Gospel. And by the way, Mr Tachibana has invited me to tea this afternoon, and before you get upset, it is at the Cathay, and I've already told Mikhail. Jack, it can't hurt to meet him. I might be able to get some idea of what he is up to."

I nodded. "As long as Mikhail and his team are there, and you stay in the hotel. See what you can get out of him. We are making some progress in tracking down MacBain," I added. I told her we had a couple of photos, and Peter and I were making the rounds of the clubs. I told her I would go out again this evening. I did not tell her that it would be to the brothels.

We were finishing our lunch of corn beef hash when Father Jacquinot walked in, and I waved him over. He took a seat, and I introduced him to Connie. He ordered a large Belgian Waffle, and then asked if I had heard the news.

"The Sanyo Towel Factory burned last night," he said. "The Japanese are saying that Chinese Nationalists are responsible, and they are threatening to send troops into Chapei to protect their citizens and property. The Shanghai Volunteer Corps leadership is meeting this afternoon at 3:00 p.m. and I will be there. If you haven't been to St. Andrew yet, Jack, I would stay out of Hongkew and Chapei until tensions ease some."

"I went yesterday, and I saw a lot of Japanese military. There was a whirl of activity at the New Asia where the Kempeitai has set up shop. I had the impression they were preparing for something."

He turned to Connie, "Miss Baker-Kerr, I cannot say I knew your father, but I knew of him. As a Jesuit, I greatly admired his scholarship and the respect he always showed the Chinese, rich and especially the poor. God grant him peace."

We said goodbye and I put Connie into a rickshaw with Josef who would escort her to her tea meeting at the Cathay. I went back to the office and called Finley, but he was in a meeting, no doubt on the mounting crisis in Chapei. I thought about calling Hollis, but he was probably tied up too, and I doubted he would tell me anything anyway. I thought who else might know what was going on and called Carroll Alcott. I told him I had some information for him, and we agreed to meet in the Cercle Sportif Francais at 4:00 p.m.

———∞———

Carroll was already at the bar when I got there. I ordered a Bombay Sapphire martini and we sat at a small corner table away from others.

"So, what have you got for me, Jack? Are we on or off the record?"

"You can use what I tell you, just don't attribute it to me. Deal?"

"Deal" and he took a pull on his drink.

I filled him in on what I had seen in Chapei and Hongkew and at the New Asia, including the fuel cans being loaded into the back of two trucks.

Carroll took another sip of his drink. "That business with the fuel cans is very interesting, Jack. I know the SMP suspects the Japs were behind both the attack on the Buddhists monks and the fire. They think the Kempeitai paid some Chinese thugs to stage the attack and then set the fire themselves. At least two Chinese members of the SMP died trying to stop the arsonists and another is in serious condition."

"Have you heard of a Special Services officer named Tanaka?" Carroll shook his head no, and I said, "The Brits think he is the hidden hand behind a lot of the violence. They claim he had a major role in the Manchuria Railway Incident. I think he or his men may have grabbed the Number One boy I told you about. It's just a suspicion. I can't prove it and the only evidence I have is a witness who said it was two Japanese who grabbed him. What the hell is going on, Carroll?"

"And Buddhists everywhere. This incident. Your client. Central Asia. You know, Jack, for a religion that practices non-violence and the Middle Way, they seem to be the middle of a lot of violent incidents." He finished his drink and set the glass on the table. "Thanks for the info, Jack. I'll keep your name out of the story. Consider yourself an 'unnamed but reliable source'. Let's stay in touch. Watch your back and stay safe."

Carroll signaled the waiter who brought over a chit. He picked it up and signed it. "Drinks are on me, Jack, besides, I'll just put it on the expense account."

I met Connie in the Horse and Hounds Bar to see if she learned anything from her afternoon tea meeting with Tachibana. She looked stressed and kept picking at the sleeve of her dress as we talked.

"He's frightening, Jack, in a way I can't put my finger on. Both Adrian and Josef were seated nearby, but I still felt vulnerable. It was nothing he said, but rather how he said it. I felt I was being interrogated however politely."

"Walk me through the meeting."

"He was already in the lobby when I came down. He had ordered two pots of tea, green for himself and English for me plus biscuits, and wasabi peas, which he ate one by one. He stood and pulled out my chair. He had a chrysanthemum pin in the lapel of his suit jacket. There was a stiff politeness about him. As we talked, I had the feeling the purpose of the meeting was to size me up rather than discuss my father's work on Buddhism. Actually, it wasn't talking. It was questions and answers, like an interrogation."

"The chrysanthemum is the symbol of the Emperor, and the pin probably means he belongs to some organization that has the blessing if not the support of the throne. What did he ask specifically?"

"There was the usual exchange of pleasantries, during which he asked after the health of my father. I told him my father had passed on and I thought I saw wheels turning in his head. He offered condolences and then quizzed me on when, where, and how, which I thought odd and it made me uneasy. He asked about father's work, and I told him I was editing his papers, which got his attention. Tachibana is knowledgeable about Buddhism, Jack, at least the Japanese varieties and their origins, so he is not a total fake in that regard, but he kept nibbling around the conversation for anything 'surprising', that's the term he used, in father's discoveries. I did not tell him about the special material he left with Ding Mu. He then asked whether the British government had shown any special interest in my father and his work. When I asked what he meant, he said whether they had examined his papers or asked about his experiences in Central Asia or were considering some recognition for his scholarship and service. And, yes, he said, 'service'. Again, it was just odd the way he asked these things. It felt like prying."

"My guess, Connie, is that he was fishing to see whether your father was in the employ of the British Government and what he may have said to them."

"I didn't tell him anything, certainly not what you told me this morning about father's possible contact with Tachibana. I tried to guide the conversation to Tachibana's background and his reason for being in Shanghai, but he ignored me and started to ask about my brother. I cut off our little meeting at that point. I thanked him for the tea and told him I had to get ready for dinner with friends. We both got up and he gave a little bow and said he hoped we would be able to talk again soon and for a longer time. I can't say he said it in a threatening way, but I don't want to see that man ever again. And, I do have dinner plans. The Crows are giving a dinner party. I'll take a taxi there and Adrian will be with me."

"I wish you'd stay in, but I doubt anyone would try anything at the Crows and as long as Adrian accompanies you there and back, I guess it is okay."

I could see her bristle. "Jack, you are not my father. I do not need or seek your approval. I understand the situation. You have thoughtfully provided bodyguards, which I appreciate, but I will live my life."

I just nodded and told her I was going to resume my search for MacBain.

There were many and varied places to look for MacBain's Sonya. Prostitution was legal and licensed in the French Concession. The International Settlement had outlawed brothels in the 1920s, but they still existed and were tolerated as long as they were quiet. Chinese singsong houses were exempt and taxed, but they catered to upscale Chinese clients and didn't use Russian girls as a rule. There were the trenches on Jukong Road in Chapei where MacBain had been rolled and robbed, so that was a possibility, but the women there looked a step or two below the girl in MacBain's photo. She didn't look like she'd be found in a 'nail shed' or lower end 'salt-pork shop', slang for the Frenchtown brothels. And Heaven knows there were many independents working cheaper hotels.

I decided my best bet was one of the upscale places. There was a house run by Mrs Maria Polunov-Morosenko, but it was in Hongkew. Given the day's events, it was probably wiser to stay out of that area and save it for later. I headed to Lotte Lester's establishment on Rue Bourgeat in Frenchtown.

I got there a little after 8:00 p.m. I wanted to be ahead of the evening clientele. Lotte was an old school Shanghai madam. I think she came here before The Great War and worked for Gracie Gale before setting up her own operation. The house—it was too nice to call it a brothel—was set back from the street in a walled yard, all the better to protect the privacy of her guests, as she called them.

There were two entrances. One was up the front steps and opened into a large foyer with a mahogany staircase that led to upstairs rooms. There was a living and sitting area off to the left and a bar with a small garden to the right and a kitchen behind that, which on request could produce a fine meal. The second entrance was around back where a hall led past Lotte's office to a second more modest set of stairs that led to the upstairs rooms. Clients in need of extra discretion used that entrance, and Lotte still had a personal client or two, and they entered that way as well.

I had called Lotte and told her I was coming by to seek her help with a case I was working. She met me at the second entrance and escorted me into her office. I had never been in it, and I was surprised. There were throw pillows and doilies, two soft chairs, a large desk with a Tiffany banker's lamp, and, the biggest surprise, a floor to ceiling bookcase filled with well-thumbed volumes.

"Don't look so dumbfounded, Jack. I don't let many people in here. It is my space, and before you ask, yes those are my books and I have read them all. I exercise my mind as well as the other parts. As I get along in years, I prefer books to people. Seen too many people. Sit down, and how can I help you?" Her smile was warm and genuine.

I took one of the soft chairs and Lotte took the other, but first poured two scotches into fine crystal tumblers and handed me one. She must have been in her mid-40s, but she had kept her figure and wasn't afraid to show it off in a gown with considerable décolleté.

"I am looking for a girl who has a relationship with a man I'm hunting because he may be able to tell me where I can find the missing person I am looking for."

"That's quite a mouthful, Jack." She leaned back in her chair and took a sip of her scotch.

I walked her through everything, Connie, Connie's missing brother, Connie's father and his ties to the authorities, the Japanese pursuit of Robin and intimidations of Connie, the missing Number One boy, all of it. I also told her that I had not shared all of the details with Connie and that in fact, I was telling her more than I had anyone else.

"Well, that *is* quite a mouthful, Jack." She leaned forward exposing a bit more of her cleavage. "Let me see the picture you have."

I handed it over and she stared at it for a bit. "She's never worked for me. She's quite striking. The smoke and Garbo-like pose looks like something Polly Grey does to advertise her girls." She rang a bell and a tall Russian appeared. She handed him the picture and asked him to show it to the girls who were in and see if any of them know her. She also asked him to check the chit records to see if a Donald MacBain had been here.

She took another sip of her drink, got up, and freshened hers and mine. "This is a hard business, Jack. I respect my clients' privacy, so you need to understand that I am making an exception in this case just by having my girls look at the picture and having Ivan check the records. I expect you to keep my confidence and I know you will, or I wouldn't have agreed to see you. We have some history, Jack, and I appreciate how you have helped me when I needed help. And this Connie of yours seems to be making a go of it pretty much alone in the world, and I know more than a little bit about that."

Thank you was all I could think to say. She was feeling philosophical, I guess, because she went on.

"This business, I don't know how much longer I'll stay in it or even stand it. White Ants knock on my door two or three times a week now. They kidnap or buy young girls and boys and sell them to brothels. I slam the door in their faces. I don't run that sort of place. I never will. I won't stoop that low." She took another sip of her drink. She shook her head. I think the drink was not her first and it was getting to her. "Conditions in the countryside must be awful. Parents selling children. I never had any, probably can't. Just as well."

Ivan came back, handed the photo to Lotte, and shook his head no. Lotte got up and walked me to the door. She put the photo in the breast pocket of my coat and tapped me lightly on the chest.

"Try Polly's. The girl in the picture looks high class. But be careful how you ask, Jack. Most of us have ties to the Green Gang for protection. Lots of kidnappings and robberies of clients. Plus, the Frenchtown police. They're worse than the Green Gang. At least Big Ear Tu's boys provide a service for the squeeze."

I kissed her on the forehead and thanked her for the drink and the information.

Polly Grey's place was even grander than Lotte's. It was a large house in the Extra Roads area. It had a cinema, gambling, and a very nice bar. The girls did not live there, but were on call when a client requested them, which is why Polly had the photos of the girls, some of them in various stages of undress.

Polly was Polish. Her real name was Sefa Stepanovna Paterson-Silipkovski. Nothing in Shanghai was simple or what it seemed. Polly had a throaty voice and eyes that could estimate to the dollar how much money you had in your pocket, not that it mattered because Polly operated on the chit system. Sign for what you want and pay her shroff when he came around at the end of the month. No one dared stiff Polly or any other madam because she would do what Gracie Gale once did to a client who declined to pay up. She dropped his signed chits in the collection plate of Holy Trinity Cathedral one Sunday.

Polly herself answered the door when I rang the bell. We walked to the bar, which was empty. It was still early. I gave her a less complete explanation of why I was there than I had given Lotte. I showed her the photo.

"Irina Svetlana Romanov. What a headache and I don't need headaches. She worked here for a while, but I had to get rid of her. She wasn't dependable. I couldn't count on her to show up and once she showed up half drunk. She liked the pipe, too. Like half the working girls, she claimed to be Russian nobility. Well, it's good for the pricing, but I think her only connection to the Romanovs would have been sleeping with their stable boy. Good riddance."

I asked Polly if she knew where Irina lived. She said she heard from one of her girls that Irina was now living in a dump, a room in Rue du Moulin near the old Chinese City.

"The area is full of Chinese brothels on the same level as the nail sheds in Chapei. Not many white women working that area, so she should be easy to find."

"Do you know Donald MacBain? Was he a client?"

"I remember him. He was crazy about her. They were made for each other. They both liked the booze and the dope."

I thanked her and left feeling for the first time that I might be getting somewhere.

CHAPTER THIRTEEN
Wednesday, January 20

The next morning I called Phil Bowman and asked him to update me on the situation with the Japanese and the Nationalists. He said the Japanese were holding a mass rally in Hongkew in the afternoon. His Marines were still at positions along Soochow Creek opposite Chapei and getting more worried about the Japanese than the Nationalists.

"Jack, the 19th Route Army is still miles to the west of the Settlement, but the Japs are building up their forces here. You saw the ships in the harbor and all the military activity around the Japanese Naval Depot. The rally this afternoon is sure to boost tensions, not only with the Nationalists but with the SMC."

"I may check out the rally, Phil."

"Be damn careful if you do, Jack. The ronin and their Chinese thugs are running wild. A couple of Marines got into an argument with some of them at the Venus Café last night. Our boys gave as good as they got, but they were pretty beat up when they made it back to the barracks. They said they were minding their own business when the ronin started pushing them. They pushed back and the next thing they knew a half dozen more Japs came out of nowhere and joined the brawl. It looks like a set up to me, Jack. In any case, the Major is howling mad at both the Japs and the Marines. He is thinking about putting the area off limits."

"Phil, do you know if Major Chin is still with the 19th? If he is, can you get a message to him? We go back a ways. I'd I like to talk to him about the situation here."

"Sure, I'll see what I can do and get back to you."

I thanked him and set off for my office where Peter was waiting.

It was a little before 11:00 a.m. when Peter and I headed out to Rue du Moulin. I figured Irina might still be sleeping off a hard night based on what Polly said. The street was near the northwest corner of the walled city. It was narrow, dank, and although part of Frenchtown, seemed part of the native city. The street was short, shorter than Blood Alley, but like it, was jammed with establishments offering women and opium. Paper lanterns were suspended over most doors and were lit when the place was open for business.

There were also some rooming houses, squat structures with one room flats, no cooking, and no baths. The cooking, if done at all, was outside on a charcoal brazier, and the street was where human waste was deposited. Sewage, opium residue, and joss sticks flavored the air. I glanced down a side street and saw an old Chinese woman skinning a rat. She smiled a toothless smile at me.

Peter approached a small boy ringing a bell and leading a blind man with a tinplate. They exchanged a few words.

"The boy says there is a white woman who lives in the building behind us. It could be Irina. He said he didn't know of any other white women."

The building had three floors with two rooms per floor. An old man sat on the bottom stair with a dozen cigarette butts on a cloth in his lap and a tin full of more. Beside him were six 'new' cigarettes. He was what Shanghailanders referred to as a 'Burlington Bertie'. He picked up discarded cigarette butts, stripped the remaining tobacco, and rolled a new cigarette that he sold to coolies. Peter asked him where the white woman lived, and the old man held up three nicotine-stained fingers and pointed to the top left room. I looked more closely at him, and I could see the jagged scar across his throat.

We knocked on the door and could hear rustling and scuffing feet. When it opened it was Irina, but far worse for wear. That lovely Garbo-like shaped face had bags under the eyes. She had on a thin silk kimono tied loosely at the waist. Her breasts were on view when she moved, and she didn't seem to care a bit. An unlit cigarette, maybe one that the Bertie had rolled, hung from her lips.

"Light. Got a light?"

Peter flicked his lighter and lit her cigarette. She took a deep pull and said, "Do I know you? Should I know you? Have I known you?" She laughed and leaned against the doorjamb, the robe opening more. "What do you want?"

I explained that I was looking for Donald MacBain and people said she might know how to reach him.

"Even if I do know him, why should I help you?'

"I'll give you US$25."

"I want $50."

I pulled two twenties and a ten from my wallet and handled it to her. "I'll be back if your information is no good."

She took another drag on the cigarette, opened the door, and said, "Look over there," pointing at the bed. A thin man with light hair and a wispy mustache lay on his back with the sheet pulled up to his waist The bed, the man, and a chamber pot were the only things in the room, besides a couple of opium pipes.

I walked over to the bed. "MacBain, Donald MacBain?" I shook him a bit and he stirred coming down from his opium high, I guessed. "Mr MacBain, I'd like to ask you a couple of questions. I'm looking for Baker-Kerr. Do you know where I can find him?"

"Robin? You're looking for the Robin the Red, Red Robin, Robin, Red Robin," and he giggled a bit. "Please forgive me, I'm tighter than usual, and the usual is tight." Donald giggled at his joke.

"Do you know where he is, Mr MacBain?" I looked over at Irina who just shrugged her shoulders and then pulled her robe closed a bit.

"He gets this way when he has had too much," she said.

"Robin, Robin, Red Robin, where are you?" and another giggle.

"Try slapping him a little," Irina said.

I just looked at her. "Donald, please try to concentrate for a moment. Your friend Robin is missing and may be in danger. I'm trying to find him. Do you know where he might be?"

"He's my friend. Red Robin is my only friend. I'm going to seed, right Irina? We're going to seed. I told him he shouldn't go, but he wanted to go."

"Go where?"

Donald sat up a bit and swayed slightly but seemed to be getting a grip. "He wanted to go west to Kansu or Ninghsia or Kashgar. Always talking about going to Kashgar. See his father's grave. Find his father's servant. Told him that was crazy. The Muslims are all up in arms, everyone knows that."

"Did he go west? When did you see him last?"

"Don't know if he went. Haven't seen him since before

Christmas."

"It's none of my business, Mr MacBain, but you need to stop this life you seem to be living. It will kill you."

I turned to Irina. "He needs to stop. He can't take care of you if he doesn't stop."

She just shrugged, the robe opening again.

I looked hard at her face. She had to be in her early 20s, but the years were starting to show. The figure was still there but the eyes were going dead.

"He'll stop when he wants to," she said. "If he doesn't, then I'll find someone else. There are many like him, and if you take your top off and get their pants down, you can get them to do almost anything." She laughed and coughed.

The speeches had already started when I got to the Japanese rally near their Consulate in Hongkew. There had to be over a thousand Japanese and the crowd was agitated. But this wasn't a crowd. A crowd mills around. This was too orderly. There were people in ranks and Japanese with colored hand paddles signaling to one another. I could see ronin around the edges leading chants and waving their arms.

I don't speak Japanese, but I recognized "shina," a slur for China. There were banners, some in English, demanding the Nationalists be punished and that the Shanghai Municipal Council protect Japanese residents. The speakers were whipping up the crowd, which responded with choruses of banzai. Pictures of the slain Buddhist monks ringed in black ribbon were on pedestals behind the speakers. A trio of Buddhist nuns were prostate before the portraits weeping loudly.

Suddenly the crowd, now really a formation, was moving. It turned on North Szechuen Road and I trailed along. The

Japanese Naval Depot was on North Szechuen, and I guessed that was where they were headed. Suddenly there was a crash, and I could see some of the ronin turning over a Chinese stall. An old lady was pushed out of the way, and then other groups of Japanese peeled off and began smashing shops and beating up Chinese. A British member of the Shanghai Municipal Police stepped in front of one group of Japanese in an attempt to turn them back, but he was hammered to the ground.

This didn't look at all spontaneous to me. It looked organized and I just decided to get out of there before things got worse when I felt a shove in my back. I turned around and there was a Japanese Major with a few ronin standing there. He had small eyes in an egg-shaped head with a slash for a mouth. My first thought was could this be the Major Tanaka I had been hearing about and warned about. The thought had barely formed in my mind when intense pain shot through my body from a hard blow to my kidneys and I dropped to the ground. I just rocked on my knees.

The Major bent down and whispered in my ear through clenched teeth. "I saw you in Hongkew on Monday. You broke the finger of one of my men. You would be wise to stay on your side of Soochow Creek because if I see you again the pain you feel now will seem mild." And with that, he slapped me hard across the face, and walked away.

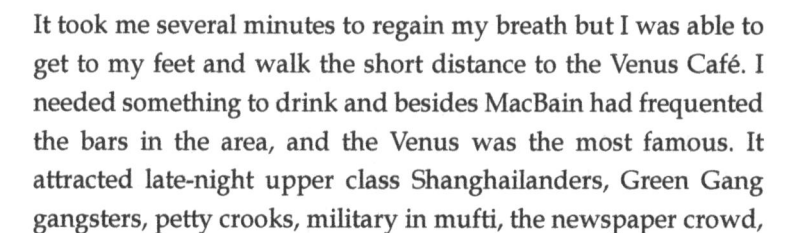

———∞———

It took me several minutes to regain my breath but I was able to get to my feet and walk the short distance to the Venus Café. I needed something to drink and besides MacBain had frequented the bars in the area, and the Venus was the most famous. It attracted late-night upper class Shanghailanders, Green Gang gangsters, petty crooks, military in mufti, the newspaper crowd, and just about every category of personage that had washed up on the banks of the Whangpoo. There were girls, of course, of every nationality including Japanese, from coasters and grifters to working girls to ladies just out slumming.

The Venus was not much to look at from the outside. The first thing I saw on entering was a sign that said, "No More Chits Accepted" and below it was one that said, "Out of Bounds to British Troops." There was no décor like at the better clubs in Frenchtown, just garish lighting.

I limped to the bar and asked if Riley was in. Riley served as bouncer and did the odd job for the owner. Some of it may have even been legal. I looked down the bar and saw he was talking to one of Shanghai's wholesale liquor distributors. I got a beer and waited for the conversation to end before approaching him.

"Hi Riley. Got a minute?"

"You look like hell. What did you do, get caught peeping some guy and his lady friend? Get fresh with some broad? I mean that's a beaut of a welt you're wearing on your cheek."

I gave him a rictus smile. "No, just a one-sided conversation with some of our Japanese friends."

"They are feeling their oats. I can't keep them out of here, of course. Besides the money is too good and for the most part they behave. But they're bad for business. People are afraid to be in the neighborhood."

"Look Riley, I'm looking for a swell and I wonder if he has been in the club. Hangs around with a guy named Donald MacBain." I handed him the picture of Robin. He looked at it for a minute.

"Who's the babe in the picture? The club can always use a broad like that."

"The man, Riley, the man. I'm looking for the man in the picture, and that is his sister, a very respectable lady. Have you seen that man? Do you know where I might find him? His name is Robert Baker-Kerr. Goes by Robin at times. He has red hair. His friends sometimes call him Red Robin."

"Respectable ladies sometimes have a shady side in my experience. Shanghai's two biggest imports are men with nowhere else to go and women carrying torches." He looked at the picture again. "The guy may have been in here. Almost everyone is at some time or another, but I don't recognize him as a regular. Can't help you with him, Jack. The MacBain guy I know. Likes his booze and he is a sloppy drunk. I've had to show him the door a couple of times."

I thanked him and left. When I got back to the office, there was a message from Phil Bowman. Major Chin would meet me at the Palace Hotel at 10:00 a.m. the next morning. I called Connie and asked her to meet me for lunch at the Cathay so I could bring her up to date. I also called Finley at Special Branch and filled him in on what I had seen in Hongkew. I didn't tell him I had been jumped by ronin or that I had perhaps met Major Tanaka.

Saudade's "he lo he lo he lo" greeted me as I came through the door of my flat. I had Lao Wu examine my back. There was a large bruise above the kidneys. I soaked in the bath for a bit and then settled into my chair with a large scotch and tried to make sense of the last two days.

CHAPTER FOURTEEN
Thursday, January 21

The Palace Hotel was across Nanking Road from the Cathay and although very nice, it was a step down from its neighbor. But it had its fans. Journalists, mid-level civil servants and military, stateless 'barons' and 'countesses'. Local gangsters also favored the place, perhaps because it was more affordable than Sassoon's monument. A friend described the clientele as "the four Fs: furtive, frayed, and financially fragile."

I waved to Tug Wilson, the manager of the bar at the Palace, when I walked in and then spotted Major Chin sitting at a small table near the back of the room. Chin was in mufti and suitably furtive, but he was a long way from frayed and there was nothing fragile about the man.

"Hello Jack," he stood and extended his hand.

"Thank you for seeing me, Te-li."

His name, Chin Te-li, certainly fit the man. Te is Chinese for virtue, energy, and principles in action, and although I was unsure which of the several characters pronounced Li was his, they all fit: sharp, clever, or strength. I had known Te-li for many years. He was Cantonese and an early follower of Sun Yat-sen and

Generalissimo Chiang. He had graduated from the Whampoa Military Academy and like Chiang had some military training in Japan before The Great War. He had attended a Methodist Mission School, so he spoke excellent English as well as Japanese and a couple of Chinese dialects. He was the head of intelligence in the 19th Route Army, effectively Phil Bowman's Nationalist counterpart.

We ordered tea and I filled him in on what I had seen in Hongkew. He said he had agents in Hongkew, and they said the beatings and looting got much worse after I left the area. The crowd marched to the Japanese Naval Depot and demanded that Tokyo deploy troops to protect them. I asked him where he thought things were headed.

"We'll fight, Jack, the 19th Route Army will fight, but I am not sure about other units." He took a sip of his tea. "You know the Canton faction forced the G-mo to resign his government posts in December because he wouldn't fight the Japanese. He is obsessed with the ragtag communists. Well, he's back. We had to back down and both factions agreed to put Wu in as Mayor of the Chinese City. Wu is from Canton, which is good for us, and he is a strong anti-communist, so that makes him acceptable to Chiang.

"But will Chiang fight the Japanese? I don't know. I know the 19th will. We are a few miles west of Shanghai and the troops are good, three divisions that are probably the best in the Nationalist army. General Tsai hates the Japs, and he is looking for an excuse to go at them."

I asked him what he knew about Tachibana, Nomura, and Tanaka. "Haven't heard of a Nomura, but Tachibana is Navy and oils his way around town moving in all the best circles. Probably Naval Intelligence. Tanaka is very dangerous, a vicious man. It's said he once had a partisan's eyes gouged out as a warning to any who opposed Tokyo's intervention in Manchuria. Many of us think he was behind Mukden Incident. I'm pretty sure he had a hand in the attack on the Buddhist monks here. He is Army and runs with the Kempeitai. He oversees the ronin and has an intelligence network too."

"What does he look like? I may have run into him."

"Medium height for a Japanese. He has an oval face and small, dark eyes. He has a mistress who was a Manchu princess. Her real name translates as 'Eastern Jewel' but she uses Kawashima here. We keep an eye on her, because she is Chinese and she's close to the puppet emperor of Manchukuo."

"I think that's who I had a confrontation with yesterday. He slapped me pretty hard and warned me to stay out of Japanese-controlled areas."

"Watch your back. I'm serious, Jack."

"What do you think will happen next?"

Chin shrugged his shoulders, a very un-Chinese gesture. "I don't know, truly, Jack. It is up to the Japs, and probably more to the Japs here than in Tokyo. The Army has been running its own foreign policy for quite a while. My guess? They'll make a series of over-the-top demands like they did after The Great War, and when Wu balks or refuses, they'll attack. That's their pattern and it has worked for them so far. But if they do, they'll face the 19th and not some local Chinese warlord with a fancy uniform and not much else."

"Do you think fighting, if it comes, will spill over into the Concessions?", I asked.

"It could, but it will certainly be on your doorstep in any case."

I thanked him and wished him well. "Take care, Jack. The temperature is rising. Watch out for Tanaka."

───∽∽───

I met Connie in the restaurant of the Cathay for lunch. She looked lovely. We ordered and I began filling her in on what I had learned since Sassoon's party but didn't mention my confrontation with Tanaka. I suddenly realized I had not seen her in two days and how much I missed her. I reached across the table and put my hand softly on hers and she let it rest there.

"We've had a breakthrough of a sort," I said. "Breakthrough may be too strong, but I found MacBain. He says Robin often talked about going to Kashgar to see your father's grave. He doesn't know if Robin went. This MacBain is an opium addict, and he rambles. I doubt he even knows where he is other than in a dump in Shanghai. He said he told Robin not to go and he doesn't know if he did. He said he hasn't seen Robin since before Christmas. Connie, did Robin ever say anything about Kashgar or wanting to see your father's grave?"

"Not in his letters, Jack, but he often talked about going to Kashgar and finding father's old servant. This is before he left England for here, so I'm not surprised he told MacBain and others that he intended to go to Kashgar."

"The situation in Chinese Turkistan is crazy, Connie. That madman General Ma is on the rampage there and the Reds are crawling all over the border area with Russia and Mongolia. I doubt Robin could even get to Kansu Province let alone Kashgar."

"Robin is Robin, Jack, and I don't think the risks would stop him from trying," she paused and added, "if he even stopped to consider the risk."

"Tell me about your father's servant, the one he left the key artifacts with. MacBain said Robin might try to find him."

"Ding Mu is more than a servant, Jack. He's like your Peter. He was with my father on all his trips. He's a Muslim and he lives in Ninghsia, in Yin-ch'uan, at least that is what my father's letter said. It would be very like Robin to try to find Ding Mu, especially if he couldn't get to Kashgar."

I sat back in my chair and my hand slipped off hers. How would Robin get to Ninghsia or Kashgar, if that was what he did, and that assumed the Japanese hadn't caught up to him and that he was still alive? I wasn't going to share that thought with Connie.

"Based on what MacBain and you have said, it seems likely Robin may have tried to go west. If he did, that means he probably went to Peking first. It's the logical jumping off place. Let me make some inquiries. Robin may still be there. When do you see Mr Chu?"

"In an hour at the Royal Asiatic Society."

"I'm going with you."

The North China Branch of the Royal Asiatic Society was on Museum Road, only a few blocks from my office and the Cathay. The Branch was almost as old as the foreign Concessions themselves. It had a great collection of Chinese artifacts and natural history items. The *China Journal* was in the same building, and Museum Road itself was as close to a cultural and intellectual center that Western Shanghai possessed. The Amateur Dramatic Club, the Lyceum Theater, the British Returned Students Union, and the Chinese Society of Science and Art were all nestled together on this short road that ran behind the British Consulate.

Mr Chu was waiting for us. He was very much the proper gentleman in his well-tailored British suit, vest, and umbrella. He held out his card. It read "Wellington Chu, Assistant Curator for Classical Chinese Documents, Oriental Library." It always amused me how anglophile Chinese seemed to make the oddest choices for their western business name.

"Miss Baker-Kerr, how nice to meet you. I am an admirer

of your father and his work. Allow me to introduce myself." All this in flawless English. "I am a graduate of St. John's, Class of 1919, and Chiao Tung University, Class of 1922. I am the Assistant Curator for Classical Chinese Documents at the Oriental Library, and as such I have the great honor to have in my care the wonderful collection of artifacts you sent ahead for safe keeping."

Connie shook his offered hand, and said, "So pleased to meet you, Mr Chu. Let me introduce my colleague, Mr Ford, who is assisting me. Perhaps we should retire to one of the small conference rooms in the back."

We settled around a small table near a window that overlooked the Whangpoo River. It was clogged with sampans as always, and despite being on the third floor of the building and back from the water, there was the faint odor of putrefaction. The tuberoses on the table did their best to cover the smell.

I sat smoking quietly as Chu and Connie discussed her father's research and the documents now in Mr Chu's care. When Connie asked if he could recommend someone to help her finish putting her father's papers in order, Chu leaped at the opportunity.

"Miss Baker-Kerr, please allow me to assist you. My training is quite good, and I have even done a cursory review of the papers, just to familiarize myself with the collection. It is quite remarkable, really. I said as much to you brother. Your father's scholarship…"

I jolted full awake. "Excuse me Mr Chu. Did you say you spoke with Robert Baker-Kerr?"

"Why yes. He came to see me not long after the documents were received by the Library."

"When was that? Do you recall exactly?"

"Oh yes, it was the first Friday in December, the fourth, I believe." He looked puzzled, "Is there an issue in discussing your father's work with your brother? I apologize if I have violated a confidence or made some other error."

I leaped in. "No, nothing like that. Robert Baker-Kerr is missing. He failed to meet his sister on her arrival, and Miss Baker-Kerr has enlisted my services in her search for him. He may be in some danger from the Japanese. We're not sure. What did you discuss with him?"

"He really wasn't all that interested in the documents, although he said that they were important and that his sister was the real expert. What he wanted was advice on how to get to Kashgar. I told him that traveling west was very dangerous, and I told him I doubted it was even possible. The Muslims are up in arms, you know. He seemed determined, however, to at least meet with his father's servant, who he said had some additional artifacts that were exceptional, groundbreaking even. I was quite excited when he said this and asked about them. He said you were the one to ask, Miss Baker-Kerr, but that they had to do with Chinese Jews and the Bible perhaps."

"Yes, Mr Chu, my father left some material with his servant Ding Mu. Father's letter suggests that he thought the documents related to the Kaifeng Jews and that one scrap may actually be a portion of the Gospel of St. Mark in Greek and Chinese."

"Oh, that would be very exciting, if so. Very extraordinary. Your brother asked if I could help him get in touch with this Ding Mu. I told him his best bet was to talk to the imam of the Little Peach Garden Mosque in the old Chinese City. He said he would and thanked me and left. It wasn't much of a conversation."

Chu went on, "You said you think Mr Baker-Kerr may be in danger from the Japanese. A Mr Tachibana came to see me the week after I spoke with your brother. He was interested in the documents but did not mention you or your brother. He asked to see the documents, but I told him that although they were in my keeping, I had not been authorized to show them to anyone. I did tell him that I expected your arrival before long and that any permission must come from you. He said he understood, thanked me, and left. It was rather odd."

Connie and I just looked at one another. I thought, how in hell did Tachibana know about the documents? He must have been tailing Robin.

I walked Connie back to the Cathay, Mikhail trailing us discreetly. I called Father Jacquinot from the lobby and asked if he could introduce me to the imam at the Little Peach Garden Mosque. He said he knew the man and he didn't speak English, so the good Father said he would come with me, but it would have to be on Monday. The imam would be tied up with prayers on Friday, and the Father reminded me that he had other responsibilities too. I decided I would spend the weekend keeping Connie company.

CHAPTER FIFTEEN
Friday-Sunday, January 22-24

It was a hell of a weekend. It started with more dark news about the growing tensions between the Japanese and the Nationalists, got a lot better when Connie and I spent time together, and ended with more bad news and a prophetic conversation with Father Jacquinot.

I checked in with Carroll Alcott Friday morning for an update. We met at Marcel, a French-style café with wonderful cakes and great coffee, not far from the French Park and the Blackstone. I told him about my witnessing part of the Japanese rally and filled him in on my conversation with Major Chin, which he promised to keep off the record. I asked him where he thought things were heading.

"I'd say there is at least a seventy per cent chance of a clash between the Japs and the Nationalists. Just an old newspaperman's sense of things, not hard data by any means. Yesterday Admiral Shiozawa issued a demand to Mayor Wu, the new Chinese mayor, and a tethered goat if you ask me. The Admiral demanded all anti-Jap activity end, including the boycott of Jap goods, the closing of Chinese papers, and rallies "offensive to the Emperor". Wu has no control like that and if he tried, the commies or some faction of the Nationalists would probably shoot him. He did the only thing he could do, stall for time by saying he would consider the demands. My guess is he will try to rein in some of the anti-Japanese groups, but it won't amount to much, even if he is sincere."

Carroll took a sip of coffee and bit into a croissant.

"Damn, this is good. The coffee and the pastries. I think I'll have another. Long night last night getting the paper to bed and then a round of the more disreputable clubs in Frenchtown. You are paying for this, right?" He took another bite and waved for the waiter to bring more coffee and pastries.

"Shiozawa was the military side of a two-prong attack. A couple of the Japanese stooges on the Shanghai Municipal Council paid a call on the SMC Chairman to express regret for the disturbances at the Sanyo Towel factory. Too bad the 'disturbances'," Carroll made quotations marks with his fingers, "resulted in the death of some members of the Shanghai Municipal Police. But they also made it clear that they expected the SMC to do something about anti-Japanese sentiment. I guess you've probably heard that the G-mo is back in full charge?"

"Yes, Chin told me Chiang was back. Chin is not sure if Chiang will fight if the Japanese push, but he said the 19th definitely will."

Carroll wiped his mouth with a napkin and said, "Let's keep in touch, Jack. We both seem to have parts of the story and I'll protect you and anyone you say is a source. Off the record or deep background, whatever you want."

I agreed, signed the chit, and we shook hands and parted.

———∽∽———

My next stop was Phil Bowman, the US regimental intelligence chief. We met in his office in Regimental Headquarters. He was as pessimistic as Alcott.

"The Brits and us are talking about what to do. Neither of us want our military getting into a shooting match between Japan and the Nationalists. We're here to protect US citizens and interests not the International Settlement. The Shanghai Volunteer Corps is supposed to protect the concessions, but the Japanese have a unit in the SVC, so how is that going to work? It's the damnedest thing. Makes your head swim when you think about it. I think everyone just wants the situation to cool but no one really believes it will. The Japs have a head of steam up, Jack. Rumors are flying that they will put troops ashore and reinforce with some more of their Navy."

"What are you hearing from your attaché in Tokyo?" I asked.

"Not much really. The civilian government is on the ropes there and the influence of the ultra-nationalists, especially those in the Army, is increasing, according to the Embassy. I don't know if the Emperor has any real power, but the Army is doing everything in his name, and he may be the only person who can restrain the military. Our Army Attaché thinks the whole Mukden Incident was cooked up and executed by the Japanese Army without the approval or even the knowledge of the Japanese Cabinet. There's not much we can do here but wait. We still have Marines manning positions along the creek opposite Chapei."

I told Phil about going to the rally and what I had seen. I also thanked him for setting up the meeting with Chin.

I said, "Chin says Chiang is back in charge but still obsessed with the Reds. He is reluctant to take on the Japs, but Chin says the 19th will fight and fight well if it comes to that."

"I have no doubt. The three regiments in the 19th are maybe the best in Chiang's army and the Generals leading the 19th know their business. I think the best the Concessions can hope for, truthfully, is that when the fighting starts, and I don't think it is an if, Jack, but when...that when it starts, it stays outside the Concessions. Of course, a lot of Westerners, including Americans live in the Extra Roads area and Chapei."

"What do you think your orders will be when the fighting starts?"

"My best guess is 'hold fast in the International Settlement'. I can't see Washington giving us orders that would lead to fighting with the Japanese. The Chinese and those Americans outside the International Settlement will be on their own and have to scamper across Soochow Creek or over the Great Western Road to get to safety. I can't see Washington doing anything for the French either. They're a bunch of corrupt bastards anyway."

On that unhappy note, I thanked Phil, told him I'd keep him posted on anything I learned, and left.

The time with Connie was wonderful. We spent part of Friday afternoon at the Recreation Grounds, even though the weather was cold, and the breeze was stiff off the waterfront. It was nice to walk hand in hand talking about anything except Robin and the situation the International Settlement faced. I was mindful that Mikhail and Leonid were somewhere observing us, but they were discreet, and I didn't care that we were not completely alone. I was just happier than I had been in a long time. She made me laugh.

We had a quiet dinner at Fiaker Café on Avenue Joffre. I tipped the maître d for a corner table away from others and had the sommelier bring us a bottle of champagne that we drank as we took time over the menu. I don't remember much of the meal itself, but Connie was radiant and relaxed. We took a taxi back to the Cathay where we had brandy nightcaps in the Tower bar. I walked her to her room, and the goodnight kiss seemed to have more feeling it in. Maybe it was the wine and the brandy.

On Saturday morning we went swimming at the Cercle Sportif Francais, which had a large, heated pool. Perhaps because it was morning, we had the place pretty much to ourselves. The Chinese pool staff was busy tidying up after last night's adventures, which must have been something. An item of lady's lingerie was tucked into the cushion of a deck chair and a shoe was in the pool. When I dropped Connie off at the Cathay, I told her I would be back at 8:30 p.m. that evening and we'd do the town.

Connie had had her hair done in the Cathay salon and she looked lovely in a pale-yellow evening gown that would catch the eye of most every man we encountered, and certainly all the women. We did some of the places we had done before. Connie especially liked Whitey Smith and Buck Clayton. We hit The Little Club and the Vienna Garden after midnight.

The Vienna Garden was the most popular Chinese nightclub. It boasted two things, Celis' All-Star Orchestra and on occasion, Tu Yueh-sheng, the head of the Green Gang and the most feared man in Shanghai. I looked around for Big Ears Tu when Connie and I entered but did not see him. If he was there, he would be in a back room.

We took a table away from the dance floor. We could still hear the All Stars, but we could also hear ourselves talk. Connie took my hand and just smiled.

"I've had a wonderful day, Jack. The swim, the salon, and I had my fortune told."

"Really?" was all I could think to say.

"It was quite accidental and a bit strange actually. Perhaps something you chalk up to the mysterious East. I was just leaving the salon when a British woman came up to me and introduced herself as Mrs Evelyn Wright, late of India, where she said she had grown up. She insisted I join her for tea in the lobby, and I thought, why not?

"She was a small woman, Jack, and I would guess in her 60s. She asked me to forgive her boldness in introducing herself, but she had a, quote, 'strong premonition that we must talk'. She then told me an incredible story about when she was age 11 an old Indian woman called on her parents and told them she, Mrs Wright, had 'the gift' and that it was the duty of the old Indian woman to show her how to use it."

"You do have my attention and please go on, but I'll order another round of drinks first. I'm not sure I can face a scary story unless I'm fortified with some more liquid courage."

Connie laughed a bit and went on. "Well, Mrs Wright's parents were apparently very broad minded because they allowed the Indian woman to visit each day and converse with their daughter about her 'gift.' This went on for about six months, according to Mrs Wright, when the Indian woman pronounced Evelyn instructed and she just disappeared. Mrs Wright never saw her again.

"I asked Mrs Wright what this had to do with me. She tells me she is able to see the future, not for everyone mind you, but occasionally the gift allows her to, and when that happens, she must share her knowledge. She called it knowledge, Jack, not a premonition or something less certain, she must share the knowledge with that person. And I, of course, asked if I was one of those persons, and she said 'yes'."

"I was trying to decide whether she was a crackpot and whether I should be amused or frightened when she launched into her, well I don't know what to call it, really. In any case, she said that she could see that I had been very concerned about some matter, but she assured me that all would be right. I asked her if the matter was Robin, and she said she couldn't tell but it was about someone close to me. She said that there was a dark presence in my life but that it was in the future. She also said there was a man in my life or would be shortly and she felt he was a good person." She smiled at me.

"I hope she was talking about me."

She squeezed my hand. "Well, I don't think it is Victor Sassoon! Although I do get the idea, he would like to see a lot more of me," she leaned back in her chair and drew her hands across her chest, "and I do mean see a lot more of me."

We danced a bit more and then returned to the Cathay.

"I have to find more permanent quarters, Jack, so I can invite you in without causing a scandal." She paused and then said, "I think Mrs Wright is right. There is a man in my life, and he is good."

———∞———

Sunday started with two phone calls. The first was from Phil. The Japanese were gearing up to make a move, he said. An aircraft carrier, a cruiser, and four destroyers had steamed into Shanghai overnight, and the Japanese had put 500 marines ashore. According to Phil, Mayor Wu had been given an ultimatum to stop all anti-Japanese activity immediately or face the consequences. They were even claiming that Chinese nationalists tried to set fire to the official residence of the Japanese Consul General in Shanghai. He said he also got a call from Major Chin. General Tsai had called a meeting of all his officers, and they vowed to the man to resist any Japanese move. "Batten the hatches, a storm is coming" was his advice as he hung up.

The second call was from Father Jacquinot who asked me to see him after Mass. I met him in his office at Aurora University. It was spartan as you would expect. There was a large crucifix and shelves full of books plus two photos, one of a family in France that I supposed was his and one of him in his uniform as the Chaplain of the Shanghai Volunteer Corps.

"Jack, I had the strangest encounter with Mr Tachibana that I want to tell you about. I ran into him quite by accident yesterday at a lecture on Eastern Religion at the Royal Asiatic Society. We only have a nodding acquaintance, so I was a bit surprised when he asked to speak with me after the lecture. We went into one of the small offices off the lecture hall, and he starts by asking me what I think of Buddhism.

"I offered some anodyne comments about it being one of the great religions and that many of its tenets and teachings were not unlike those of Christianity. He said that is so and then began an elliptical digression on the history of the Jesuits in China, the dispute with the Franciscans, Pope Clement XI, and what all. It had me wondering, 'What this is all about?' I have to admit that Mr Tachibana knows quite a bit about religion in China.

"He then said that he was interested in the history of Buddhism, especially the Pure Land and Zen sects, and their spread from India to China to Japan. He told me that he had been part of Count Otani's third expedition. He asked me if I knew of the work that Sydney Baker-Kerr has done, and I told him that I knew Baker-Kerr slightly but was unfamiliar with his scholarship.

"He appeared disappointed at that and said he had heard that Mr Baker-Kerr had made some very interesting discoveries and he wondered if I had heard the same. I said no. I felt like I was being interrogated, although his manner was never brusque or threatening. I decided to turn the tables a bit and asked him as a practicing Buddhist how he reconciled that with his military career. That's when the conversation got really interesting. Maybe strange is a better word.

"He said there is no conflict and asked if I was familiar with D. T. Suzuki, the Zen philosopher. I knew the name and I knew he was a favorite of the ultranationalists in Japan, but I said no. Tachibana told me that he is a great admirer of Suzuki, and that Suzuki explains that when Japan fights, it is really an expression of Buddha's compassion. He must have seen the puzzled expression on my face because he launched into a more detailed explanation. It was so incredible that I wrote it down afterwards."

He pulled a piece of paper from his desk drawer.

"I have it here. 'Zen teaches the gospel of love and mercy, and so when a true practitioner is drawn into war for reasons unrelated to his ego, he is not responsible for the behavior of his sword. Indeed, it was not the true practitioner that did the killing but the sword itself. The true practitioner has no desire to harm anyone, but the enemy appears and makes himself a victim. The sword performs its function of justice automatically, which is the function of mercy.'"

I was as befuddled as Father Jacquinot. "You think he really believes that?" I asked.

"Oh yes. I don't know what he wants with Baker-Kerr, but he is part of the ultranationalists driving Japanese policy in China. He was quite open about that and quite proud of the fact. He said that Japan's diplomats are not part of the Emperor's Way and that they are really gilded peacocks strutting in their cage, fanning their feathers for show, and having little influence. He was critical of the Japanese Army and made clear that in the opinion of the Navy, the Army has made a mess of the campaign in China, but Japan would prevail and end colonial oppression in Asia.

"I fear war is inevitable, Jack. It is just a matter of time. Of course, the war has already started in China, and the West won't escape it. I think the Japanese Army will find the Chinese a tougher piece of meat than they expect. They can control the coasts and the major cities, but the countryside is too big and the Chinese too many for them to ever be safe. The Chinese are a proud people, and they will not cave. I am sure of that."

We just looked at one another for a minute and neither of us knew what to say. We agreed to meet the next morning at 10:00 a.m. and then proceed to the Little Peach Garden Mosque. I rose, thanked him, and left for Saudade and her cheerful 'he lo he lo he lo."

CHAPTER SIXTEEN
Monday, January 25

I met Father Jacquinot after morning mass at Aurora University and we took a rickshaw into the old Chinese City. On the way, Father Jacquinot gave me some background on the imam and Chinese Muslims, the Hui.

"How do I address him, Father?"

"Call him imam Ma, his title and surname. I know him a little bit. The Little Peach Garden Mosque isn't as grand or wealthy as the mosque in Sung-jiang south of the city, but the imam is very respected, not only among his congregation, but more broadly across Shanghai's missionaries and clerics. He also is an excellent source of information on what is happening in the Muslim areas in the Northwest. The mosque's worshipers mostly come from that area. He doesn't speak English so let me handle the conversation."

"I could have asked Peter to come along."

"The imam is more likely to talk if a Chinese isn't there. What do you want to know precisely?" He stressed that last word.

I told the Father I want to know if Robin had visited him and when. I said I wanted to know what the imam told Robin and if he knows where Robin might be. All I got was a nod and the Father slipped into what I called his game face—flat expression, air of dignity, no hint of what he was thinking or feeling—as the rickshaw pulled up in front of the mosque.

The Little Peach Garden Mosque sat in a rectangular courtyard on the east side of which was Chinese-style building that Father Jacquinot told me contained offices and a reading room. The imam's quarters were on the south side facing west toward Mecca. Chinese characters and Arabic lettering in green decorated the entrance to the mosque.

Father Jacquinot asked a young boy in the courtyard to tell the imam that we were here, and he came back in a few minutes. With some hand motions he directed us to a small garden near the imam's quarters. The imam was tall for a Chinese, probably 5'9" or so and had a white wispy beard and warm dark eyes. He was Han Chinese, I thought, and not one of the Muslim minority peoples from the west. Father Jacquinot had told me Islam came to China sometime in the seventh century during the Tang dynasty, like Buddhism, probably from Persia via the Silk Route.

The imam stood to greet us and asked us to join him at a small table in the garden, where a servant poured tea and provided small plates of dried seeds and fruit to nibble on. Father Jacquinot did not translate as we went along but stopped periodically to give me the gist of the conversation. There was apparently an exchange of pleasantries, some small talk about their respective work among their parishioners, and then Father Jacquinot went through why we were there, summarizing the events of the past week without dwelling on the Japanese angle.

The imam spoke for several minutes, and I guess Father Jacquinot could see how anxious I was getting because he paused the conversation, apologized to the imam, and then summed up things for me.

"The imam says Robin did come to see him. He wanted his help in getting to Kashgar. The imam told him politely in so many words that it was crazy to try. Robin wouldn't hear of it and said he would try to get there anyway."

Apparently, the imam understood more English than he let on because he interrupted Father Jacquinot and told him in Chinese that Robin was a rash young man who should respect the advice of elders. I knew enough Shanghai dialect to know that Father Jacquinot said he couldn't agree more.

Father Jacquinot returned to summing up the conversation. "The imam said that Robin said if he could not get to Kashgar, then he would go to Ninghsia and find Ding Mu. The imam advised against that too, because General Ma is a psychopath, and he is slaughtering people across the region. The imam proposed a solution, which Robin reluctantly agreed to. The imam would contact Ding Mu using his people and ask Ding to travel to Peking to meet Robin. He told Robin to contact Imam Na Li at the Ox Street Mosque in Peking."

"When was this conversation? And does he know if Robin went to Peking?"

There was another exchange and then Father Jacquinot explained to me that the conversation had been in early December, and the imam did not know if Robin went to Peking. He said he did get word to Ding Mu. Ding sent word back that he would try to get to Peking and that he would bring some special items left in his trust by Baker-Kerr.

I asked the imam if he would give me an introduction to his contact in Peking as I planned to go there and look for Robin and Ding Mu. He agreed and I thanked him. I started to get up to leave when the imam stopped me. "He has a question for you, Jack," said Father Jacquinot.

There was another exchange between the two men and then

Father Jacquinot turned to me. "He said he is very concerned about the tensions between the Nationalists and the Japanese. He said he heard this morning that the Manager of the Mitsui Bank branch on the Bund presented a list of grievances to the Shanghai Municipal Council on behalf of all Japanese residents in Shanghai. The Japanese are demanding an apology, an indemnity, and the punishment of all who assail Japanese citizens. The imam wants to know what you think. Will there be fighting? He is showing you great respect by asking your opinion, Jack, so give it some thought. This isn't polite conversation."

I paused and then said, "Tell the imam that I share his concern. Although a compromise might be possible, I believe it is likely there will be a clash. I hope it's short and I hope the Concessions and the walled city are spared, but any fighting could easily escalate and spill over. The walled city is Chinese territory in any case and is not protected by treaty like the Concessions. I do not think the Japanese would hesitate to pursue Nationalist soldiers into the walled city, and if they do, many innocent people will die."

Father Jacquinot translated. "He thanks you for your assessment, Jack, and he agrees with it. He especially fears for the refugees outside the Concession. He hopes the Japanese would respect the churches and temples and mosques because places that belong to God ought to be refuges, but he fears the Japanese do not think that way. I told him I shared that view and that perhaps the religious leaders in Shanghai should meet to see what we might be able to do. He agreed."

I thanked the imam again and we headed back to Frenchtown.

———∞———

I met Connie at the Horse and Hounds. "I have a lead on Robin," I told her. "There is a good chance that he is in Peking."

"Peking? Why is he in Peking?"

"Well, I am not sure that he is, but it is a lead. I spoke to the imam at the Little Peach Garden Mosque. He said Robin came to see him, just as Mr Chu suggested. Robin asked about getting to Kashgar, and the imam dissuaded him. I'm afraid the imam does not think much of your brother. Too impetuous and not appreciative of the wisdom of his elders."

"That's Robin, alright. Where in Peking? Did the imam say? Why did he go to Peking? He was supposed to meet me." She started out sounding relieved but now I could see she was getting angry.

"Connie, I'm not sure he is in Peking. He may be and it is the only lead we have. I'll work on it. The imam talked him out of trying to get to Kashgar by offering to send word to your father's old servant and ask him to meet Robin in Peking."

"I don't think Robin would have waited to hear from Ding Mu. He would have gone directly to Peking to wait, maybe even try to get to Ninghsia. He is just so damn rash!"

The strain of the last few weeks was getting to her, and her stiff upper lip was giving way to the emotion beneath the surface. I guessed it was a mixture of genuine concern for his safety and deep resentment at his behaving the way he had.

"All this was in early December, so the timeline fits with what we know about when Robin was last seen. I can go to Peking to look for him, but I hate the idea of leaving you alone here. Things are going to explode."

"No, you must go! I have Mikhail and his companions. I'll be safe with them watching over me. Jack, Robin is all the family I have left," she paused and then said, "and he is a thorn in my heart". She looked like she was about to cry. The words came more quickly now. "I've always looked after him and I can't stand the thought of losing him. You said the Japanese may be after him. He is probably in danger. I want him to be safe. I want to be safe. He is all I have left. I have no father, no mother, just my brother and my father's work. It is all I have left. Robin is all I have in this world, Robin and my father's work. They mean everything to me."

I could see tears starting to form in the corners of her eyes. That tells me where I stand, I thought. It must have shown in my face because she put her hand on my arm and said, "I don't know what I would do if I didn't have you. You are my knight-errant," she said with a half laugh. "Please find him."

"I'll go to Peking but let me do a little digging to see if I can't locate him or at least narrow the search. I'll call Alan Mowbray at Astor House and ask him to check the better hotels in Peking. See if Robin is staying in one. It will take a day or two. If Robin is there, we can wire him to stay put, and I'll go to Peking to escort him back."

"What if he isn't in one of the hotels? What then?"

"Then I'll go to Peking and find him." I was tempted to add "if he is there" but thought better of saying it out aloud. She squeezed my arm harder and mouthed, "Thank you so much."

She excused herself and went to the ladies' room. I waved Mikhail over. I told him I was off to see Alan Mowbray and asked him to tell Connie where I was going and that I would see her tomorrow.

CHAPTER SEVENTEEN
Tuesday-Wednesday, January 26-27

Alan was more than happy to help. He said he would make discreet inquiries through his contacts at the major hotels in Peking. He warned me that it probably would take a couple of days. I thanked him and went to my office where an invitation was waiting for me.

The invitation was for tiffin at the British Consulate at 1:00 p.m. The Consulate sat on immaculate grounds at the juncture of the Whangpoo River and Soochow Creek. The Public Gardens and the band stand, where Mario Puci led the Shanghai Symphony in better weather, were across the road. And the great ocean liners and the warships of various powers were anchored along the river. Pier 1 was always reserved for His Majesty's Navy.

The wind off the river was stiff and cut into me. A brief shower in the morning had left the road slick and the air was heavy and damp. As I got out of my rickshaw just before 1:00 p.m., I saw Hollis leaving the grounds. He stepped into a black sedan and sped away.

Tiffin was not the only thing, or even the most important thing, on the menu. The meeting was about the Japanese and the escalating tensions with the Nationalists. As the other guests filled in, I wondered why I was there. The Brits were well represented and at the most senior levels, and that didn't include Hollis who obviously had been there earlier. There was the British Consul General, the Superintending Consul, the Commander of the British Forces in Shanghai, the British Commissioner of the SMP, and the Major who led the British unit of the SVC. The US Consul General was there along with Fessenden, Phil Bowman of the 4th Marines, and Finley of Special Branch. Jardine, Swire, and the Hongkong and Shanghai Bank were well represented, as were key foreign allies of the Brits and Americans. The attendees were also notable for who was not there. There were no Japanese and no French.

That was a surprise, but not as big a one as seeing Major Chin in the room and the head of the Green Gang, Tu Yueh-sheng. I had only seen Tu from a distance a few times or in a photo when he was honored with a place on the French Municipal Council. But that was Tu alright, a slight man in a long black silk gown with white cuffs turned back at the wrists. He had the gray, pasty skin of a prolonged opium user, and it was tight on his face. The eyes were small and very black and his neck barely extended above his collar. His hair was close cropped, and his large ears stood out from his head and gave him the nickname no one uttered to his face, Big Ears Tu. The hands were bony with long nails that curved. He always reminded me of Nosferatu, but Tu was real and far more frightening. A large Chinese man stood next to Tu but slightly behind him. He was obviously a bodyguard, but he leaned in from time to time and whispered in Tu's ear. He was also translating for him.

We were ushered into a long formal hall where a table was laden with various Western and Chinese dishes. We were invited to fill our plates and make our own drinks as the Consul General had dismissed all the staff and servants. He quickly got down to business.

"Thank you for coming on short notice. I know how busy we all are, but I believe the present situation with the Japanese demands our attention," he said and added after a studied pause, "and our cooperation. I think most of you know one another, but I want to be sure to introduce a few people who some of you may know of but may not have met.

"We honored to have here with us Major Chin Te-li, head of intelligence for the 19th Route Army. I am equally honored to welcome Mister Tu Yueh-sheng, one of the most influential members of the Chinese community and a great Chinese patriot."

I thought the description was British understatement and diplomacy at its best. Tu was a key ally of Chiang Kai-shek and had helped him crush the communists and the left wing of the Nationalists in 1927 when Chiang turned on his former compatriots in Shanghai. Chiang also had the quiet approval of the SMC, which turned a blind eye to the movement of Chiang loyalists through the International Settlement to attack the communist strongholds north of the city and did nothing to rein in the Green Gang as it butchered Chiang's new enemies.

"I also want to welcome Mr Jack Ford." I was shocked by the sound of my name, and it must have shown because he quickly added, "Mr Ford is known to some of you in the police and intelligence circles. He has been closely monitoring Japanese activities over the last week, including the activities of the ronin, and since this meeting is about the Japanese and their...the polite word would be auxiliaries, I thought he ought to be here.

"And I'm sure you have noted the absence of our Japanese and French Shanghailanders. I must stress that this is a secret meeting and that you are not to speak of it to anyone who is not here. The reason the Japanese were not invited should be obvious. I chose not to include the French because they tend to go their own way and, in all frankness, I do not trust the current French administration."

He then turned to the British Commander of the Shanghai Municipal Police and asked him to bring the group up to speed on the developments of the last few hours. He was brief and precise in recounting events without interpreting them or judging them.

"Gentlemen, let me tell you what we know as of now and what we believe may occur over the next few days. Admiral Shiozawa has assured the SMC that Japan will not violate the neutrality of the International Settlement. This assurance," I could hear the skepticism in his voice, "came after the commander of the Japanese Marines threatened to march into the Settlement and close down the pro-Nationalist Chinese press. Mayor Wu is trying to stall the Japs who have demanded he put an end to the anti-Japanese boycott. The Defense Committee will meet this evening, and of course, the Japanese and the French will be there. In short, gentlemen, the pot is on the boil and the only question is when it will boil over, not if."

The Consul General then asked Major Chin what he thought. Chin was equally succinct. "I think Wu will declare martial law, and the Generalissimo is meeting with his advisers. The 19th Route Army will fight if the Japanese attack."

He went around the room asking each person in turn how they saw the situation. There was no disagreement with what either man had said. When he came to me, he asked what I thought the ronin would do. "The ronin will go after prominent Nationalist citizens, certainly in Chapei, but perhaps in the Settlement, too, kidnapping them or assassinating them. They will operate behind the lines spreading terror however they can."

Tu's bodyguard coughed briefly, and all eyes turn on him. "Master Tu says we, too, know how to operate in the shadows."

Those cold eyes left no doubt that that was true.

Things continued to deteriorate on Wednesday. As Chin predicted, Wu declared martial law and the Generalissimo convened his Council of Advisers. Afterwards he dispatched 1,500 troops to Shanghai to help Wu with the crackdown. The Japanese upped their pressure tactics, including pressing Western journalists to write articles supporting Tokyo. The Japanese mill owners called on the Navy to protect them and their property, and Shiozawa said he would. At the Defense Council Meeting the previous evening, Shiozawa promised to give the SMC twenty-four hours' notice before taking action. That evening the Japanese Counsel-General gave Wu an ultimatum: all anti-Japanese activity must end by 6:00 p.m. the next day.

I telephoned Alan to see if he had heard anything from his Peking contacts. He told me Robin had checked into Le Grand Hotel de Pekin and hadn't checked out, but it was clear he had not been in his room for several days. Alan offered a number of possible explanations from being on a bender to falling prey to the Japanese.

"Thanks Alan. I think I need to go to Peking and see if I can find Robin or discover more."

"The area around the North Train Station is a beehive of Japanese military activity, Jack, and the ronin are active too. I think some Nationalists forces are also beginning to take up positions. If I were you, I'd leave from the South Train Station if you can, and get to Peking that way. It's longer but you are less likely to run into any Japanese."

"Thanks again, Alan. That makes sense. Do you have a contact in Peking who might be of help?"

"Not really. Just hotel security, but I'll give you an introduction.

His name is Dubois. I don't trust him entirely. The Nationalists hold on Peking is weak and the Japanese are pressing hard. You never know who's on whose side, so be careful."

I rang off and sent Peter to buy a ticket on the 6:15 a.m. train to Nanking. I called Connie and offered to fill her in on what I had learned and my plans. She suggested dinner in my flat and I quickly agreed.

Lao Wu had a cocktail set laid out when Connie and I walked through the door. We were greeted with a jubilant "he lo he lo he lo" from Saudade. I could smell dinner being prepared and it was one of Lao Wu's Northern Chinese delicacies. I made us each a martini and we sat together on the couch. She put her head on my shoulder and I took in that clean smell I noticed when she first walked into my office three weeks ago.

Over dinner I recapped everything I had done over the last two days. I told her that Robin was in Peking and that I was taking an early train tomorrow to look for him. I did not try to hide my concern but said we shouldn't jump to any conclusions either. I could see she too was concerned, but that British resolve was on display. After dinner we were back on the couch with another drink.

"Connie, I am very concerned that the fighting will spill over into the Settlement. I'd feel better if you stayed here for the next few days. I'll be in Peking and Lao Wu can make up the guest room."

"That's not necessary, Jack."

"Please, Connie, stay here."

"You misunderstand, Jack. It is not necessary to make up the guest room." She leaned in and kissed me softly on the lips.

CHAPTER EIGHTEEN
Thursday-Friday, January 28 and 29, Peking

Peter drove me to the station the next morning. I told Peter to make sure Mikhail kept a close eye on Connie, and I told him I would cable him from Peking every day.

The station in Shanghai had been quiet and I did not detect any surveillance, but it was there when I stepped onto the platform in Peking shortly after 8:30 p.m. I couldn't tell if the two likely ronin were waiting for me specifically or just on duty watching the comings and goings for their military masters. I had one small bag and asked the porter to get me a rickshaw. I thought about trying to shake any possible surveillance, but it was getting late, and besides there were only a couple of places a western traveler could go, and the Japanese were sure to have those staked out or have hotel staff on their payroll. I told the puller to take me to the Grand Hotel de Pekin.

Shanghai was vibrant, modern, gaudy, and the future of China. Peking was scholarly, sedate, and the past. Peking had the remnants of the old Imperial retinue, the universities, and tradition. If Shanghai was glitzy, Peking was drab by comparison. It had been my first posting in China when I came with the

Marines, but I never really got to know the city.

Like Shanghai, Peking was a city of pieces. There was the old Tartar City with its high walls and gates, the Forbidden City that was the Emperor's former compound within the Tartar City, the old Legation Quarter, which like the Concessions operated independently even if it wasn't supposed to, and the greater, sprawling Chinese City, with its endless mazes of alleys called hutongs. Covering everything was a fine cloud of dust blown in from the Gobi Desert just to the north.

The Northern Warlords had fought for control of the city in the 1920s, and even after Chiang and the Nationalists took control in 1928, rival generals still tried to make the place their private fiefdom while pledging allegiance to the government in Nanking. As the rickshaw wound through traffic to the hotel, I could see a sizeable Japanese presence in the city.

The Grand Hotel de Pekin was on the north side of the Legation Quarter and lived up to its name. It was seven stories of pinkish granite that offered a panoramic view of the Forbidden City from its top floor restaurant. Being French, the dining and wine list were unmatched in the city and perhaps all of China except for the Cercle Sportif Francais. The lobby was high-ceilinged and pillared with polished wood floors in a large checkerboard pattern. Fine carpets took you from the entrance to the desk and then to the grand marble stairway. A small bar was off the lobby, and because George Bernard Shaw had frequented it during his stay, it was known as the Writer's Bar.

I made my way to the front desk and asked for Mr Dubois, who turned up as I finished registering. We shook hands quickly and then he guided me to a corner of the Writer's Bar. He was a small man, well-dressed, and sported an Adolphe Menjou moustache. He was as wooden as his surname implied and every bit as silent as an oak. I ordered two brandies in the hope of warming him up. When they arrived, I went quickly through my story of looking for Robin on behalf of his sister and asked if he had any idea where his guest might be.

"There is very little I can tell you, Mr Ford. Mr Baker-Kerr checked into the hotel in mid-December for an extended stay. He paid in advance through the end of this month. That is a bit unusual but not unheard of. Doing business here these days has become more... complex, shall we say?"

"When did you see him last?"

"I'm not sure. He has not been in his room as far as we can tell since the middle of last week when the maids changed the bedding and straightened the room."

"Don't you find that strange? Were you concerned? Did you contact the authorities?" My frustration evidently was beginning to show because Dubois's manner became icier.

"Monsieur, nothing is strange in Peking these days. People go about their business for their own reasons, and it sometimes takes them out of town or away. Mr Baker-Kerr is paid up through the end of the month, he is a quiet guest, and I have reason to inform the authorities, and then there is the question of which authorities to inform. I suppose the British? What about the Chinese? The Japanese?"

I just gave him a look. This was obviously not going anywhere, and he was being purposely difficult. "I'd like to look around his room. It would comfort his sister and perhaps I might see something that could help me locate him. You or your representative, of course, would accompany me."

I could see his face tighten and consider rejecting my request, but he apparently decided that the best way to get rid me was to let me see the room.

"Very well, Mr Ford. I will accompany you. For his sister's sake. Please follow me."

Robin's room was on the third floor at the back of the hotel. The room was small but elegantly furnished with a large bed, desk, and upholstered chair. There was a cabinet that doubled as a chest of drawers and liquor cart. There wasn't much of a view from the single window, but you didn't take the room because of the view. It was clean, safe, comfortable, and convenient.

Dubois stood just inside the room as I headed to the bathroom. Robin's shaving gear was still there along with all the usual toiletries. I opened the closet in the main room, and it was full of clothes. His suitcase was inside the door on the floor. The chest held shirts, socks, and underwear. He clearly had not intended to be out overnight, let alone for ten days.

I pulled open the drawer in the nightstand. A box of .38 caliber shells was open and two-thirds full, but no gun. The desk was clean. I ran the tips of my fingers over the notepad by the phone but there were no indentations. If he had written something down, he had taken it with him and the couple of sheets of blank paper beneath it.

I thanked Mr Dubois and returned to the lobby to pick up my room key. But before going back upstairs, I sent a cable to Peter. "GET MIKHAIL HERE FASTEST STOP COME PREPARED STOP." My quick search of his room convinced me that Robin had gone to meet someone whom he did not trust, was probably armed, and expected to return the same day. The latter hadn't happened, and I wanted Mikhail armed when he arrived.

I was surprised to see Mikhail in the lobby the next morning when I went down to check messages at the front desk. There was a sinister looking Chinese man in long black gown and fedora with him.

Mikhail saw the look of surprise on my face and said. "We

flew. You said fast. I have never flown before. It was exciting. This is Mr Chan, who is a friend of Mr Tu. Mr Tu strongly suggested that Mr Chan join us. Peter told Tu that you needed help."

I didn't know what to say other than ask them to join me at breakfast. We took a table in the corner where we could speak privately. I saw a couple of Japanese with close cropped hair and loose jackets, like they were carrying pistols, observing us from across the room. I quickly brought Mikhail and Chan up to speed on my conversation with Dubois and the search of Robin's room. I asked Mikhail what had happened in Shanghai since I left.

"All hell has broken loose, Jack. The fighting has started, I'm sure. Yesterday morning, the Japs warned the Consulates they would take action in twenty-four hours if the Chinese didn't cave to their demands. It had the opposite effect. The 19th Army started to move into Chapei and take up defensive positions. The Japs countered by moving more Marines into Hongkew. The SMC declared a state of emergency and martial law and called out the SVC to defend the settlement. Chinese students and workers began demonstrating against the Japs, and the Japs started to move troops into Chapei. We caught a night flight, and as we headed north, I could see gunfire around the Woosung Forts."

I sat back, and asked the question that was foremost in my mind, "How's is Miss Baker-Kerr?" I could see that Mikhail knew she spent the night at my flat and side-stepped the question.

"She spent most of the morning at your flat before joining Carl Crow for lunch at Sun Ya. Adrian was with her the rest of the day and the evening. She and the Crows were headed to the American Club for the evening when I boarded the plane."

He read the look on my face. "She's in safe hands, Jack. Adrian, Leonid, and Josef have her surrounded and she is cooperating with us."

I just nodded. "I'm going to the Ox Street Mosque to find an imam Na Li, who Robin was supposed to contact here. I think there is a good chance I will be followed. I would like you two to counter-surveil me. If I am being tailed, don't interfere unless you think they are going to try to attack or kill me. I think the Japs are more interested in who I might see than in me personally, but you never know."

We finished eating and a half hour later I left for the Muslim quarter of Peking by rickshaw. The two tough-looking Japanese in the corner left as we were getting up.

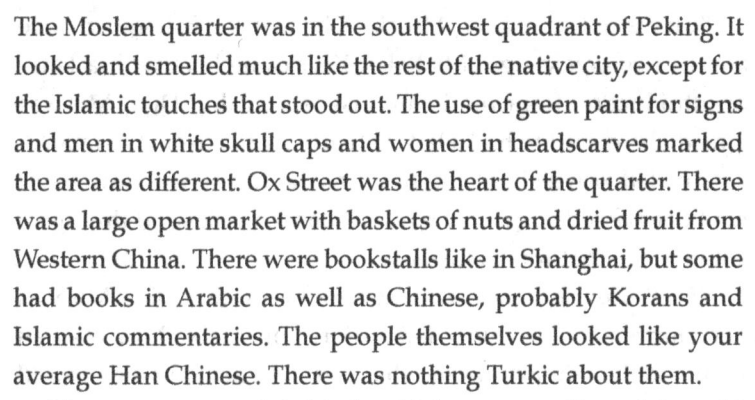

———∞———

The Moslem quarter was in the southwest quadrant of Peking. It looked and smelled much like the rest of the native city, except for the Islamic touches that stood out. The use of green paint for signs and men in white skull caps and women in headscarves marked the area as different. Ox Street was the heart of the quarter. There was a large open market with baskets of nuts and dried fruit from Western China. There were bookstalls like in Shanghai, but some had books in Arabic as well as Chinese, probably Korans and Islamic commentaries. The people themselves looked like your average Han Chinese. There was nothing Turkic about them.

The mosque stood behind a high stone wall, and I could just make out the green tiled roof above it. I walked through an arched doorway into a quiet and beautiful courtyard. Straight ahead was the main mosque with the characteristic arches and a minaret. Off to the side were two flanking pagodas in Chinese style. Quite a contrast.

I walked up to an ancient man sitting on a bench by one of the pagodas, introduced myself, and handed him the letter of introduction imam Ma had given me. He looked at it and motioned for me to sit and wait while he walked slowly off.

A few minutes later a tall Chinese in a white skull cap and flowing robe walked up and said, "I am Na Li. I was expecting you. The imam sent word ahead that you would be coming." He had my letter of introduction and what looked like a cablegram in his hand. He motioned for me to follow him, and we went into a small room in one of the pagodas. Tea, nuts, dried fruit, and red bean rice cakes were on a small table. We sat down and he poured tea.

"How can I help you, Mr Ford?" His English was excellent.

I went quickly through the bare-bones version of my story — helping a sister find her missing brother — and asked if he could help me find Ding Mu.

"I have not seen Ding Mu since he met Mr Baker-Kerr here almost two weeks ago. Mr Baker-Kerr came here with a letter of introduction from the imam just as you did. Ding Mu was already here. He too had a letter of introduction from the imam." I marveled privately at the reach of the imam and how word could be passed so quickly over a thousand miles and through a countryside that was in turmoil.

"I left them to talk privately. I could see that Ding Mu was very moved to see young Baker-Kerr. They talked for over an hour and then they came and thanked me. They said they would be back later that evening and they left. That is the last I saw of either of them."

"They didn't return, then?"

"No."

"Do you know what happened to them?"

"No, I've had no word and I made some inquiries. I'm afraid that some misfortune has occurred."

"Do you know where they may have gone? Anything would be helpful, a direction or general place."

"They did not say. But Ding Mu did say that he had something for Mr Baker-Kerr that Mr Baker-Kerr's father had left in trust with him. So, I assume they went to wherever Ding was staying in Peking."

"Do you have an idea where that may be?"

"No, I am sorry. I can only surmise that it is with relatives or people who came here from his home area of Ninghsia. It will be in the hutongs."

"What does Ding Mu look like?"

"He is a small man of about 60 years or more I would guess. He is slightly stooped and walks with a stick. He is a good Muslim. He has a white beard and wears a skull cap. I am sorry I cannot be more precise."

"Thank you, imam Na. You have been very helpful, and I appreciate you taking the time to see me."

"May God help you, Mr Ford. And may you find Mr Baker-Kerr safe and healthy. Inshallah."

"Yes, inshallah."

I took a rickshaw back to the hotel and met with Mikhail and Chan. I recounted my talk with the imam and asked if they had any idea on how we might find Ding Mu.

Chan spoke quietly but with force. "If he is in the hutongs, I will find him. Please, we will know by morning."

I could only nod and thought the imam Ma wasn't the only one with a network that spread across vast distances and could reach into any corner.

"Was I followed?"

"Yes." It was Chan again. "They will not bother us again."

CHAPTER NINETEEN
Saturday, January 30, Peking

The phone in my room rang at 4:30 a.m. I jerked awake. I hadn't been sleeping much anyway. "Yes?"

"Jack, this is Mikhail. Chan knows where Ding is staying, and he believes Robin is with him. Get dressed and meet us at the side entrance to the hotel. There is surveillance, but Chan's colleagues are on them."

We walked, and in two blocks we were in the labyrinth that was the hutongs. I had no idea where we were. Chan seemed quite sure as he never stopped to get a bearing or check a landmark. Human waste, garbage, cooking smells, and damp all mixed. There was little sound beyond dripping water, but people were beginning to stir, and I could hear a baby start to fuss. We had been walking for twenty minutes or so when Chan stopped in front of an archway that led to an inner courtyard with a half-dozen or so doors.

Chan walked to the third one on the left, tapped gently on the door, and spoke softly. I heard the name Ding Mu and then Lao Tu, probably a reference to Tu Yueh-sheng. The door opened and a weak light from a lantern bled into the courtyard. Chan spoke again and the door opened wider. I could see an elderly Chinese gentleman with a whitish beard and a skullcap. I thought this must be Ding Mu. Chan stepped aside and motioned for Mikhail and me to go in.

There was no light except for the lantern. It was really just a single room with a table, some chairs, a cooking area with a red paper kitchen god pasted to the wall, and a traditional Chinese brick bed with a frightened white man on it holding a knife.

I spoke quietly but firmly, "Robin, Connie sent me. I'm going to bring you back safely. My name is Jack."

There was doubt in his face, but he lowered the knife and leaned back.

Ding spoke, "He has been shot through the shoulder and he fell when we were getting away. I think he may have some broken ribs."

I looked at him. His eyes were closed. There were beads of sweat on his face and his slacks had a tear in the knee. His red hair was plastered to his forehead. Blood had seeped through the bandage on his shoulder, but it was dry. Maybe the wound had closed. I walked over and laid my hand on his forehead. It was hot and he jerked awake and pulled the knife up again. I took it from him and gently pushed on his good shoulder until he was once again lying on his back.

"Who are you?" he asked.

"My name is Jack Ford. Your sister asked me to find you. She is very worried. She expected you to meet her at the pier."

"I was here," he said. "How do I know you are telling the truth? Some people tried to kill us."

"Your sister gave me this." I handed him the photo of Connie and him. "She told me you were called Red Robin at school because of your hair. I know your father was a respected China scholar and explorer. I know Ding Mu was his servant and that your father left some special items of historic importance with him. And I know you came here to meet Ding and that the imam at the Little Peach Garden Mosque helped you, just as he did me."

"Okay." He winced with each breath. The ribs I thought. "I believe you. Besides if you were part of the gang that tried to kill us, you would have come in firing."

"I need you to rest while we figure a way to get you back to Shanghai and safety."

I turned to Ding and asked him what happened.

Ding motioned for us to sit on a small bench. Mikhail and I took a seat and Chan stood guard at the door. He had a pistol out and I saw him wave three fingers at the courtyard. His men must be out there.

"I met Mr Baker-Kerr at a tea house in the Legation Section of Peking. I recognized him easily because he looks very much like his father. When we left to come here to get the scrolls his father left in my care, we were followed. Just as we got to the hutongs, one man opened fire. The bullet missed us, and I turned to see three, maybe four men, running toward us. The second shot hit Mr Baker-Kerr and he went down. I picked him up and we hurried into a side alley and then another. We lost them but Mr Baker-Kerr stumbled and fell very hard against an archway. That was when he hurt his side. I got him up and we made it here. This hutong is mostly Muslims from Ninghsia. A doctor of traditional Chinese medicine stitched and bandaged the wound and gave me some herbs to make a special tea for him."

"When was this? Are men still hunting you?"

"It was the middle of last week, I think, and yes, men are still hunting us. Ninghsia people are hiding us. They say it is the Japanese that are looking. I was afraid to move Mr Baker-Kerr. I was unsure who to turn to for help."

"Thank you Ding. I am most grateful, and I know Mr Baker-Kerr's sister will be, too. Can you get the doctor to come? We need to get out of here and you should head back to your home if you can. I'll take over from here."

"I'll send for the doctor."

I reached into my pocket for some money, but he stopped me. "I do not want money. I was his father's servant and assistant. He always treated me as an equal, not as a coolie. I helped bury him in Kashgar and I hope one day to go back there and sweep and tend his grave. I have fulfilled my promise to him to keep the scrolls safe and see that they reach his family. I deeply regret that I could not protect his son." He turned and walked out the door. I never heard from him again.

The Chinese doctor changed the dressing on Robin's shoulder, and I got a look at his side. It was badly bruised and swollen. Unlike Ding, the doctor spoke no English and Chan had to translate.

"The doctor thinks the ribs may be broken but he cannot be sure. The bullet went straight through. He was lucky that it did not hit bone and splinter. He advises rest and his special teas and the compound of herbs he put on the shoulder wound."

"Well, we can't wait here. Not with the Japs looking for us. Sooner or later, they will find someone who can point them in our direction. The train is out of the question. The Japs will be all over that and the airport too. That leaves boats and cars."

"Boat would be a smoother trip than a car on Chinese roads." Mikhail said.

"Yes, but we'd have to get him to Tientsin to get him on a coastal steamer and the Japs are likely to be all over those too."

"I can get a car." It was Chan.

I didn't bother to ask how. Chan was certainly a man of impressive resources, and I knew if he said he could get a car, there would be a car.

"Okay, car it is. It gives us the best chance of evading the Japanese and getting out of Peking. Let's hope there are no roadblocks or bandits."

"I will get two cars. One for my men and one for us. You and I will take turns driving. We'll not stop. Mikhail can tend to our ill passenger."

"How long will it take to get the cars, Chan?"

"A few hours. My men will have food and water in the cars. You need to prepare Mr Baker-Kerr for the journey. I will be back when it is dark, and we will leave then."

I scribbled a note and handed it to him. Cable this to Miss Baker-Kerr at the Cathay Hotel: "SUCCESS STOP RETURNING SOON STOP." He nodded and with that slipped out the door into the growing light of morning.

Robin was awake. "How's the pain," I asked. "We are going to drive to Shanghai. It's over 800 miles. We're going to do it straight through. It's likely to be bumpy at times but it gives us the best chance of avoiding the Japs who are hunting you. Do you think you can handle that?"

"Yes." He looked puzzled. "Why are the Japs hunting me?"

"I'm not sure. They either want what you have, the scrolls, or they are afraid of what you may know. Maybe both. But they are after you." I thought better of telling him that they were sniffing around Connie, too.

"Can you clean me up a little? I have some clothes at the hotel."

"We can't go back there. We'll have to travel as we are. We'll make you as comfortable as we can. Can you sit up?"

We helped him to the edge of the bed. I could see the pain in his face from the ribs. He didn't complain. I had to hand it to him, he was tough. While we waited for Chan and nightfall, Mikhail and I rigged a stretcher for Robin from a couple of bamboo poles and an old blanket. We'd have to carry him to the car. As tough as he obviously was, he was in no shape to walk out of the hutongs to the street and the car.

CHAPTER TWENTY
Saturday Night, Sunday January 30-31

Chan was back shortly after sundown on Saturday. Mikhail and I carried Robin on the stretcher, and it was about 5:30 p.m. when we exited the hutongs. There were two large Buicks parked on the street. There were three men in the second car, no doubt Green Gang colleagues of Chan. We eased Robin to a standing position by the first car and then gently folded him onto the backseat. There was a sharp intact of breath, the pain must have been awful, but he didn't say a thing. Mikhail propped him next to the door and we put the stretcher on the floorboard in the back. I got behind the wheel and we were off.

It was cold and dark, and the wind was howling off the Gobi. That was good because there were fewer people out and we were able to make good time. We covered the eighty miles to Tientsin in under two hours. We skirted the city and followed the old Grand Canal to P'i-chou, Kiangsu Province. We arrived there a little after 2:00 a.m. Sunday.

Chan and I had been switching off every couple of hours, and it was my turn behind the wheel again. Chan had stocked the cars with a first aid kit, dried fruit, and large thermoses of hot tea. Robin was sleeping fitfully in the back seat and Mikhail had his eyes glued to the road behind us. The second car was keeping pace.

We made Soochow not long after the sun came up. It had been sixteen hours on the road without a real break. We were only seventy miles or so from Shanghai, but we were also nearing the battle zone north of the city. I pulled off the road and the second car followed.

Soochow was almost due west of Shanghai but slightly north. The question was how best to get back into the city. One option was to drive south and go in that way, but that would add hours to the trip and Robin's wound was seeping again and he was running a fever. Chan thought it might be possible to get through via Jessfield in the northwest corner of the Settlement. We didn't know what the fighting situation was, but it had been concentrated farther east in Chapei and Hongkew, according to Mikhail. The Buick had a radio and we turned it on to get the news. We picked up a local Chinese station and Chan listened for a bit.

"Chiang has ordered the 5th Army to Shanghai to reinforce the 19th Route Army. They came through here yesterday. There was a cease-fire, but it broke down. The situation is confusing. The fighting has been very heavy around the North Train Station. The Japanese have bombed Nationalist positions in Chapei, but the Nationalists are holding firm according to the radio. There are many fires. The Chinese trade unions have called a general strike at the Japanese-owned mills and there have been many clashes with Japanese soldiers."

"Can we get in through Jessfield?" I asked.

"I don't know. The radio says there is heavy fighting, but it seems farther East."

I thought a bit. We decided to try that way. As we moved

CITY OF LOST SOULS

down the highway, we could see smoke far off in the distance. The land is flat here and the fires must have been twenty miles away, but they were big.

We started to encounter Chinese peasants moving north and west away from the general area of Shanghai. Many were pushing wheelbarrows or pulling carts with a few belongings piled on top. Children who could walk were tied together behind parents or conveyances while babies were strapped to mothers' backs or piled on top of the belongings. Some had bandages. There were also bodies along the roadside of those who were too injured or too weak to continue. They were probably refugees from the floods and fighting in Kiangsu last year who had settled in squatter camps north of the Concessions. They were on the move again with even less hope than before. We weaved our way through the diaspora, but the numbers just increased.

Chan was driving when we encountered the tail elements of the 5th Army and the roadblock. Three soldiers stood in the road at port arms, and a lieutenant judging by the green shoulder boards with two stripes was signaling all traffic onto a side dirt road headed north and away from the city. There were a few vehicles and trucks ahead of us and all turned off and headed north.

When we reached the soldiers, Chan tried talking his way though. I caught a few words, ch'ing-pang and Tu Yueh-sheng, the Green Gang and Big Ears Tu, but the names made no difference to the lieutenant who only repeated "bu neng tso" or 'cannot pass' several times before ordering the soldiers to point their rifles at us. We pulled onto the dirt road heading north.

It was early afternoon now and I had only the vaguest notion of where we were headed. The road was a rough dirt track and Robin groaned with every bump. Chan was driving slowly and at least there were fewer refugees. The little traffic ahead was moving slower than we were, however. I had Chan pull off the road and the other Buick followed us.

Mikhail, Chan, and I got out and they lit cigarettes. "Any idea where we are," I asked, "or how we can get help for Robin and into the city?" Chan called the other Green Gang members over and they chatted for a few minutes. Then he came over to me.

"I believe we are not far from Monument Road. It runs very close to Soochow Creek. When we cross the creek there will be people to help us."

"Okay. I know where that is. Monumer becomes Pearce and that runs along the creek toward Jessfield."

We got back in the cars and headed northeast until we came to a road that seemed to be heading due east. We turned off and while the road was in no better shape than the one we had been on, there was less traffic, and we could move a bit faster.

We also stood out, however, and that was when the plane spotted us and came in firing. I couldn't see if it was the Nationalists or the Japs, but the machine gun bullets marched up the road at us and I ducked beneath the dash. The first bullets went through the hood and the roof and caught the second Buick full in the windshield. Chan pulled off the road and we scrambled out, Mikhail pulling Robin who screamed in pain. We rolled into a ditch beside the road as the plane made a second pass. I could see the Rising Sun on the wings now. It put several more rounds in our car and the second Buick caught fire. Chan and I ran to it, pulled open the left side doors. The driver was dead and slumped over the wheel. We pulled the two other men out and one was bleeding from a small cut on his head. I couldn't tell if it was from the wreck or a bullet.

We all piled into the ditch and waited. The pilot apparently was satisfied with the damage done and left. "Who's hit?" I asked. The wound to Chan's man was a cut when his head hit the dash and that was all. The other Green Gang member was shaken up but unhurt. A bullet had gone through Mikhail's coat, but he was unhit. Chan and I were okay, but Robin's shoulder was bleeding again.

The cars were done for. One was on fire, and I could see water pouring out the holes in the radiator of the other. Mikhail dashed to our car, pulled out the makeshift stretcher, the first aid kit, a couple of thermoses, and the sack of food.

We laid Robin on the stretcher, and Mikhail opened Robin's shirt and lifted the bandage. The stitches were in place for the most part, and he applied a new bandage on top of the old and used pressure to try to stop the bleeding. It worked after about a half hour. "Lots of practice in the White Army," he said. Robin had passed out and was sleeping.

"I think we better wait here until its dark before we try to move. It will only be a couple of hours," Chan said.

Chan signaled to the man with the cut forehead, gave him some orders, and sent him off. "He will be back after dark."

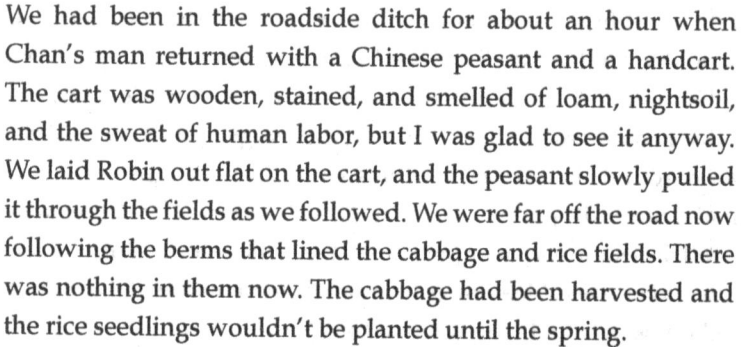

We had been in the roadside ditch for about an hour when Chan's man returned with a Chinese peasant and a handcart. The cart was wooden, stained, and smelled of loam, nightsoil, and the sweat of human labor, but I was glad to see it anyway. We laid Robin out flat on the cart, and the peasant slowly pulled it through the fields as we followed. We were far off the road now following the berms that lined the cabbage and rice fields. There was nothing in them now. The cabbage had been harvested and the rice seedlings wouldn't be planted until the spring.

The moon was a waning crescent and threw little light, which was probably just as well. The peasant knew his way, and I was concerned that the Japs or Nationalists even would open fire on a half dozen people making their way across dark fields in the middle of the night. The going was hard, and we were all very tired. The ground was uneven, and I fell a couple of times and was lucky that I didn't twist an ankle.

After a couple of hours, it must have been after 3:00 a.m., and we approached a road. It didn't look big enough to be Monumer or Pearce, but it was paved. Chan signaled for us to drop to the ground while he scouted ahead. He was only gone a few minutes when he returned with an all-clear. We hurried across the road and were again on the berms. Then we were at the edge of a creek, and there was a small boat there. It was shallow draft and had a plank deck with a lean-to structure of canvas and a small storage area below the aft deck. Chan lit a match, cupped a hand around it, and then raised it twice. An oil lamp flickered on, went out, and we scrambled aboard.

We carried Robin from the cart to the lean-to and covered him with a filthy canvas cover. The rest of us huddled on the deck. The boatman's wife brought bowls of rice with some pickled cabbage. We hadn't eaten much since leaving Peking, and we all wolfed down the food. Robin was still out, and we saved a bowl for him.

When we finished eating, Chan, Mikhail, and I weighed our next move. Chan suggested we stay put and sleep while he sent one of his men ahead to get more help and learn what the situation was like up ahead. That sounded like a great plan to me. We all crawled into the lean-to and lowered the flap, and I was soon fast asleep.

CHAPTER TWENTY-ONE
Monday, February 1, Outskirts of Shanghai

I woke about mid-afternoon. The boat was still tied up where we had boarded it. Robin was awake, and Mikhail looked at his wound and changed the bandage. Chan was nowhere to be seen, but I suspected he was off contacting other Green Gang members. His man hadn't returned, and the man with the head wound was standing guard.

Robin was hungry and I took that as a good sign. He ate the rice and cabbage and drank heavily from the thermos of tea. I asked him about the pain, and he just nodded. The kid was a lot tougher than I expected. He was alert and rested enough to talk.

His first words were "Where are we?" followed immediately by, "How did I get here?", "Who are you?", and "How is my sister?"

"One at a time," I said. "First, you are with friends. I think we are on Soochow Creek somewhere west of the Concessions. Major fighting has broken out between the Japanese and the Nationalists. We are holing up here until we can figure a safe way into the city, and the Japanese are looking for all of us." He leaned back against the side of the lean-to and took another sip of tea. I lit my last cigar.

"My name is Jack Ford. I was hired by your sister to look for you. I've been doing that for three weeks. Why didn't you meet her when she arrived or leave word where you were?" There must have been some irritation in my voice because he glared a bit before answering.

"I thought I'd be back in Shanghai before she arrived, but it took longer to find and meet Ding," he stopped and switched his train of thought, "Where is Ding? Is he okay? We were attacked by Japanese."

"Ding is safe in Peking. You probably owe your life to him. He got you some medical help and looked after you. Like I said, Connie and I have been looking for you for three weeks." He seemed surprised and a bit taken back when I referred to his sister as Connie.

"I was able to trace you through your friend MacBain and the imam at the Little Peach Orchard Mosque. I followed you to Peking and through Na, we found you and Ding. I had help. Mikhail works for me." I pointed to him, and Mikhail nodded. "Mr Chan, who isn't here at the moment, has," I paused and thought how best to describe him and then said, "many connections and he was key to finding you in the hutongs and arranging our escape."

"The Japs have been looking for you and they have their eyes on your sister, too." I saw him give a start. I held up my hands. "She's safe. I have bodyguards with her, and she is with friends in the Concession. I don't think the Japanese will bother her. I think they hoped she would lead them to you. They're more interested in you and me. We've had a couple of brushes with them in Peking."

I stopped talking and asked him, "What happened to you?"

"I went to Peking to meet Ding Mu. I wanted to go to Kashgar to see my father's grave, but that was impossible, and then I wanted to go to Ninghsia instead to find Ding. But that was impossible too. I guess things are very bad out west."

He stopped and took a painful breath before continuing. "The imam in Shanghai helped me to contact Ding. I met him at a tea house in the Legation Quarter, and he told me he had some special things my father asked him to keep safe until Connie or I could collect them. We had just entered the hutongs when two Asian men stepped in front of us and three came up behind. They were about twenty yards ahead and behind, and I could see they were armed."

I could see the strain on his face and I told him to take it slowly. He nodded.

"When the man in front started to pull a gun, I pulled mine and fired twice. I'm a good shot and I hit him, and I saw him spin around and chips from the wall of the hutong cut the face of one of the others. Ding pulled me into a side alley, and we started to run. That's when I got shot. I felt the bullet go through my left shoulder. I went to ground and lost my gun. Ding helped me up and pushed me down a narrower pathway. I stumbled and mashed into a corner of a wall. My side hurt like hell, but I kept moving as quickly as I could, and Ding just took corner after corner. It's a maze in there and we lost them. We got to his place, and I collapsed and passed out. When I woke up my shoulder was bandaged and there was a compress of some foul-smelling mixture on it. I don't know how long I was there."

"Over a week," I said. "Do you know why the Japanese are after you?"

"I haven't the slightest idea. I knew a few Japanese in Shanghai and we always got along. I'd see them at the Cercle Sportif Francais usually and we'd have a couple of drinks before we went our different ways. I just don't know why they'd want to kill me."

"Did you ever meet a Tachibana or a Major Tanaka?"

"I had drinks with Mr Tachibana of the Japanese Consulate a few times. He is quite an authority on Buddhism. He had heard of my father and asked about his work. I told him I just knew father was very interested in the early history of Buddhism, but that I never could get interested in that stuff myself. I told him my sister was the real expert on my father's work."

"Well, that helps explain his interest in Connie," I said. "Were you aware that your father had a relationship with the British government, the security services in particular?"

"Father?" He chuckled, "No. He just seemed entirely engrossed in his scholarship. I find that hard to believe."

"Well, I think he had some sort of relationship, perhaps just passing on to the Government anything he observed in his travels that might bear on British interests in India and Asia. Robin, may I call you Robin?"

"Oh, yes. My sister told you that is what she called me?"

"Yes and call me Jack. We're in this together and now is no time for formality. Here's what I think, and it's speculation, but it makes as much sense as anything. I think the Japs, Mr Tachibana and Major Tanaka, specifically, think your father was working with the British military or security people and that he saw something during his travels that the Japanese did not want him to see or report." I thought about sharing a bit of the conversation I had with Hollis but thought better of it. "Tachibana was in Chinese Turkistan the same time as Sir Aurel and your father. Did Ding say anything to you about your father's death?"

"Only that he died of fever in Kashgar."

"Nothing about encountering Japanese explorers or monks?"

"No."

"Whatever the reason for hunting you, I guess it doesn't

matter." All at once I thought to ask about the whereabouts of the items Ding was holding for him.

"Oh, Ding sewed them into the lining of my coat when we got to his place. He thought that would be safest way to carry them. It is just a few fragments of three scrolls and some loose pages of Greek stuff with some classical Chinese text."

"That's good." I paused. "We'll talk more later. You need to rest before we move again. The Japs are probably still looking for us, and we need to get you back into the International Settlement and to hospital."

"What happens next?" he asked.

"Chan sent a man to scout ahead, and we need to wait for him to come back. I'm not sure exactly where we are except that that we are on a creek still well west of the city and the fighting. For now, we stay put."

He nodded, settled back, and was soon asleep again.

———∾∾———

Chan's man was back a little before sunset, and he had copies of the *North-China Daily Herald* from the last three days. The front-page photos were horrible, flames and smoke billowing from across Soochow Creek in Chapei. The stories, if anything, were worse.

While I was enroute to Peking, Admiral Shiozawa was warning the diplomatic corps that Japan would take action in twenty-four hours if the Chinese did not meet their demand that the Nationalists shut down all anti-Japanese activities. This sent the SMC into a tizzy. It declared a state of emergency and called out the SVC to defend the Concession. The American Consulate also asked Manila to send 400 more US Marines to Shanghai.

Meanwhile the 19th Route Army was digging in in Chapei even as the Chinese Mayor accepted the Japanese demands.

This touched off rioting by Chinese students and workers who roughed up some Japanese nationals, according to Tokyo. In early evening Shiozawa ordered Japanese troops into Chapei and the Japanese began shelling the Woosung Forts at the entrance to the Whangpoo River. By midnight the battle was on, according to the *North-China Daily Herald*.

When the Japanese marched on the North Train Station on January 29, they encountered stiff resistance from the 19th Route Army and were forced back. The Japanese started setting fires to buildings as they pulled back. My heart sank when I read that one of the buildings was the Commercial Press. Connie's father's life's work, except for the material sewn into Robin's coat, was in the Commercial Press Oriental Library, which was across the street from the main Commercial Press building. I said a little prayer under my breath that Mr Chu had managed to get the crates to safety.

The British and American Consulates tried to get both sides to agree to a three-day cease fire that would allow civilians to be evacuated. It went into effect at 8:00 p.m. on the twenty-ninth but broke down almost immediately. The Nationalists had an armored train that they drove into the North Station railyards and used it to bombard Japanese positions. The Japanese started bombing and strafing runs, and it was clear from the papers that thousands of civilians were trapped in the war zone. The fighting so far had been outside the Concessions, but I was worried that it would spill over. The *North-China Daily Herald* reported instances of stray rounds crossing Soochow Creek, and the 4th Marines had turned back some Japanese soldiers trying to get behind Chinese lines by crossing into the Settlement.

I couldn't stop thinking about Connie and the fires at the Commercial Press. I decided not to say anything to Robin, because there was nothing we could do, and I didn't want him more distraught than he was. All I could think about was getting back into the city and looking after Connie.

Chan came back about 9:00 p.m. bearing news, some of which was more depressing than the press accounts I had read. Most disturbing was the fact that we were not on Soochow Creek, as I thought, but on a northern tributary well past Jessfield and closer to Chapei and Woosung. The road we took east must have been farther north than any of us realized. And that wasn't all. Chan had been in touch with his Green Gang buddies and the news was bad.

"My friends have joined the fight. The Japanese control the main streets but we control the alleys. Snipers are taking a heavy toll on the invaders. The Japanese are killing civilians and setting fire to buildings to clear out the snipers. They opened up with machine guns down Broadway yesterday trying to kill snipers but only killed civilians. Women and children, it makes no difference."

"Can we go back toward Jessfield and get around the fighting?"

"No, I am afraid not. The Japanese are launching a major offensive tonight or tomorrow in Jessfield area to protect their cotton mills and to set up artillery on the flank of the 19th Route Army. The Americans and British are trying to arrange a ceasefire. We can cross into the Concession when it goes into effect. I have men who can guide us from here and hide us in Chapei."

I looked at him like he was crazy.

He said, "We are on Yu-ching creek. You know it. It flows past Hongkew Park and joins the Whangpoo near where Soochow Creek enters the river. We will stay on this boat until we are near Pao Shing Road in Hongkew. We will be met there and taken to a safe place by my people, and we will wait for a chance to cross into the International Settlement."

My mind was a jumble. It sounded crazy but I couldn't think of anything better. And Chan's people had brought us this far and had proven incredibly resourceful. Robin needed a doctor soon, and the farther we could go by water the faster and easier it would be.

"Can you get a message to Robin's sister and Father Jacquinot?" I asked. "I want his sister to know he is alive, and I want Father Jacquinot to know what our plan is. Do not tell Robin's sister he is hurt but do tell Father Jacquinot. Can you do that?"

"Yes. We know and respect Old Do Things. He is a good man."

"Robin's sister is Miss Constance Baker-Kerr and she is staying at the Cathay."

"We will contact her."

Chan called over his man and gave him his marching orders. Then he turned back to me.

"I've sent a man to do as you ask. My other man will stay here. The boat is too small for all of us. I will stay with you until we get to the safe place. We must not be seen. Some of us will have to stay below deck and the rest in the lean-to but covered up. The Japanese have their spies among our people and a boat with Westerners on it is sure to attract attention if we are spotted. The boat people do not travel at night, so we will leave just before dawn."

Chan produced two .38 Smith and Wesson revolvers. I had my .45. Mikhail had the Nagant Revolver he had carried as a Czarist officer. Chan handed one of the .38s to me and said it was for Robin. He kept the other.

CHAPTER TWENTY-TWO
Tuesday, February 2, Chapei

Boat was a generous way of describing the skiff we were on. It was flat-bottomed and had a shallow cargo area at the back where Mikhail, Chan, and his man all huddled beneath a tarp. There was the lean-to contraption that sheltered Robin and me, and it was where the family normally slept. The boat was propelled by a poles manned by the husband and wife, who was heavy with their second child. A baby was strapped across her chest. How they survived and what they did to earn a living was beyond me.

We pushed off as the sky was beginning to glow in the east. In the daylight I could tell we weren't on Soochow Creek. This little stream was too narrow, and I could tell by the sun that we were heading south-south-east and not more easterly. The winds are mostly west to east, so the smoke from the fires in Chapei were drifting away from us. But they were heavy, and ash and soot soon started to fall on us. I could see the glow of the fires and could hear the thud of artillery. I couldn't tell if it was Japanese or Nationalist, probably a bit of both. My high school Latin flashed in my mind: Aeneas on his way into Hades and this was the River Styx.

There were other small boats on the creek, but most were just stationary. There was no reason to go forward, although that was what we were doing, and there was nothing for these people to go back to. I could see squatters and refugees in make-do shelters along the banks of the stream. They had fled the fighting and were now trapped here.

The sound of gunfire became louder as we slowly made our way downstream toward the junction with Soochow Creek. I didn't see any soldiers, but Japanese aircraft were in the air and strafing anything that moved. They occasionally shot at the boats in the stream. These people were not part of the fighting, and they were doing nothing other than trying to survive. I felt myself getting angrier especially after corpses, many of them women and children, started bumping against the side of the boat.

In early afternoon we poled to shore near some shanties a few yards away. These were more permanent-looking structures than the refugee camps we had passed, and I could see pathways and allies between them. I still had no idea where we were. I only hoped it was somewhere near Pao Shing Road. Chan sent his man scurrying over the side and toward the shanties. He kept low and was soon out of sight.

Chan had changed from his silk gown to peasant clothing and came and stood next to the lean-to. "We'll wait here until dark. I've sent my man ahead to get help caring for Mr Baker-Kerr. "

"Where are we? Near Pao Shing Road?"

"No. We are near the border of Chapei and Hongkew. We have more friends here."

I didn't ask. I took it he meant more Green Gang men. My doubts about the wisdom of all this were growing, but there was nothing I could do about it. Besides, I told myself, so far so good. Nothing I could do but trust that our luck and his connections would get us through.

CITY OF LOST SOULS

We were much closer to the fighting now. All the boats had put out their lanterns so not to attract attention or gunfire. As night began to fall, I could see the tracers more clearly. If you didn't know better, it looked like red rain or the sparks from caldrons when they pour liquid steel out. The noise of artillery and small arms was louder as it became darker, and the glow from the fires was reflected on the underside of the clouds overhead. The artificial light from the fighting cast a soft glow on the area around us, and I could get a better idea of where we were.

The Yu-ching was running east and west, so we still had to be some distance from the point where it turned north and south. That meant the road I could see just to the south of the stream had to be Liu Ying, so we were not all that far from Pao Shing Road.

As dusk turned to night, Chan's man and two others approached the boat after signaling Chan with a lighted match. The two men had bamboo poles and when they got closer, I could see that they had improvised a stretcher for Robin.

"We leave the boat now," Chan said, and Mikhail and I dropped over the side and waded the few yards to the bank. The two men stood in the water while the boatman and his wife helped Robin onto the stretcher. I saw Chan hand a red packet of money to the boatman who put his hands together in front of his face and bowed quickly two or three times. A Buddhist, I thought. Chan slipped over the side and joined us on dry ground.

Robin grunted as the two Green Gang men struggled to get up the slippery bank. There was another artillery flash and some flares, and we were lit up momentarily. The moon's waning crescent was all the light we had. Chan barked something in Chinese and the two men moved out quickly in a crouch toward the shanties. We did the same and covered the thirty or so yards in a few seconds. We ducked into one of the alleyways between the shanties and stopped to get our breath. A third man stepped out of the shadows, and I raised my pistol before Chan put his hand out and pushed it down.

"This is our guide." Chan and the man spoke quickly in Chinese, and then Chan turned to me. "There are many Japanese patrols on Pao Shing Road so we will stay in the alleys. There is a safe house near North Honan Road. We have more men, food, and a doctor there. There is heavy fighting in the area, but we will stay in the alleys and keep North Honan Road on our left until we get close to Yung Shing Road. We will assess the situation when we get there. We will have to cross Yung Shing to get to the safe house. Once there, we will rest, treat Mr Baker-Kerr's wounds, and wait. There will be a pause in the fighting, and we will cross into the International Settlement. Once in the International Settlement we should be safe. After we cross Soochow Creek on the Markham Bridge, it will be easy to get a taxi there to take Mr Baker-Kerr to Lester Hospital. Rest for a few minutes and then we will move out. I want to be in the safe house before dawn."

I stopped myself from thinking how crazy this was by chambering a round in my .45.

The going was tougher and much slower than I expected. I glanced at my watch when the sky was lit by flares.

It was after 3:00 a.m. and I don't think we had gone more than a half dozen blocks, but it was hard to tell because the alleys twisted and turned, and we had to stop every few minutes and scout the way ahead. Chan's man would disappear for several minutes, then return and we'd move forward another forty yards or so.

CITY OF LOST SOULS

When we got to where Hung Shing crossed Tien Tung An Road it was almost dawn, and I got my first clear look at the fighting. We went to ground in a courtyard off Tien Tung An. I crept forward with Chan's man to scout the way ahead while the others huddled against the interior courtyard wall.

The area had seen some heavy fighting, although things were quiet at the moment. The houses off the courtyard had apparently changed hands a few times. There were bodies of both Nationalist soldiers and Japanese lying about. The fighting must have been hand-to-hand at some point because several had bayonet wounds and even in the dim light I could see powder burns on tunics. The stench was awful. They had apparently been there a day or two and were unburied because this was no-man's-land.

The worst, however, were the civilian casualties. Among the many was a dead Chinese mother lying face down with a dead child under each arm. Her blouse had been ripped off and there were slash marks across her back and legs. Samurai sword, I thought. One child's head was nearly severed from its body. I turned and vomited against the wall. I wiped my mouth on my sleeve and Chan's man pulled me forward.

We low crawled to where we could see down Tien Tung An to Hung Shing. Barbed wire was strung across Hung Shing just ahead of the intersection with Tien Tung An. I could see Japanese soldiers behind sandbags. They had a Type 11 Light Machine Gun, a trench mortar, and a Type 91 howitzer with large wooden wheels. The buildings along Hung Shing were all pockmarked by shells, and many were in ruins. Debris filled the streets. I could see burned out cars and overturned rickshaws. And bodies, civilians judging by their clothing. Apparently, the Japanese strategy was to destroy everything in their way, regardless of who or what.

I saw a muzzle flash in the upper story of a ruined building on Hung Shing and the impact of the round in one of the sandbags. Sniper. The Japanese opened up with the machine gun and howitzer and poured rifle fire against the building. A second and third sniper round rang out but from a different part of the same building. There was either more than one sniper or the sniper was moving from location to location after each shot to avoid Japanese return fire. Maybe both. The Japanese kept up fire for over a minute until an officer carrying a samurai sword ordered ceasefire. There were no more rounds from the building. The sniper or snipers had moved on or were dead.

We crawled back to the others in the courtyard. There was good news. I knew where we were, and we were only few blocks from the intersection of Hung Shing and Yung Shing Roads where the safe house was supposed to be. The bad news was obvious. We were in the middle of the battle and the Japanese were busy securing the area, and judging by the civilian bodies we saw, killing anyone they came across.

"Well, what now, Chan?" I asked with some irritation in my voice after I told him what we had seen. "It looks like we are in the middle of it. We sure as hell can't go backward, because Robin needs attention, and I don't see how we move forward. The sun is up, and we are sitting ducks if we move." Just then, as if to underscore my point, the area to our front and left erupted in fierce small arms fire.

We all flattened ourselves against the wall. I could hear and, I swear, feel rounds hit the other side of it. Bits of brick and grout rained down on us, and a large piece of the wall collapsed, just missing Robin.

"We have to move," I shouted, and kicked Chan's guide in the leg. "Get us out of here now." It was plea, order, wish, and desperation. He crouched low and started to move along the wall. I waved the stretcher bearers forward and Mikhail grabbed

Chan and pushed him ahead.

There was a moon door entrance to the courtyard, and we sprinted past it, still crouching, as fast as we could. One of the stretcher bearers went down, and Robin thudded to the ground in the open. He gave a muffled cry and a groan, and Mikhail grabbed his jacket collar and dragged him from the opening. The downed bearer was finished. The right side of his head was gone and there was a neat hole under his left eye where the round had entered.

We regrouped on the other side of the opening. Fire was coming from in front of us and behind us. The Nationalists were attacking the Japanese strong point on North Honan Road. I heard the swoosh of a mortar shell being fired and it exploded behind us and to our left. I couldn't see the combatants, but their fire fight concussed all around us. Then it stopped as quickly as it had begun. Silence, the sound of a few rounds, and then silence. I looked over at Robin. His breathing was ragged and he was holding his side, but he was quiet. My respect for him grew.

Chan signaled with his hand to follow, and we moved out staying low in a file. Mikhail picked up one end of the stretcher with Robin on it, and he and the other bearer went next. I brought up the rear. We moved along the courtyard wall. We were probably visible to anyone in one of the upper stories of the buildings along Hung Shing, but we had no choice. I prayed, I really prayed, that if there was anyone in those buildings, they were more interested in the Japanese than us.

We entered an ally and I felt safer for the moment. It was very narrow and dark, and we moved quickly until we came to a major cross avenue. Chan put up his hand and we stopped. I went forward and crouched beside Chan. The buildings on this street were pocked marked, too, but the street itself was clear. I started to stand to see better when Chan grabbed the back of my shirt and pulled me down. Then I heard what he evidently had, engines. A Vickers Crossley armored car with a rising sun on the door turned the corner and headed down the street. It was followed by three open trucks filled with Japanese soldiers. They were headed toward the strong point I had seen on Hung Shing.

Like most streets in Chapei, this one was not wide, and it was lined with stores and alleys that led to cheap housing in the back. Thirty yards or so to our front was the Tailors' Guild Building, and it was pretty much intact except that the front door was off its hinges. That was good. Like most Chinese buildings there was a screen a few feet behind the door and at a right angle to the entrance. Good feng-shui. Evil spirits travel in a direct line and can't turn corners. If we got to the building, the screen would conceal us and there had to be at least one other entrance and exit at the rear.

I pointed at the Guild Building and Chan nodded. I waved Mikhail up and explained to him that we were going to dash across the street and enter the Tailor's Guild. I told him Chan would go first, then he and the bearer should follow immediately with Robin, and I would bring up the rear. The street itself was quiet, but we could hear gunfire from back where we were. Chan peeked cautiously out and then sprinted to the door. No gunfire. I waved Mikhail forward, and then we were all across and inside the building, where a new horror awaited.

The Japanese had apparently used it as an interrogation and holding area. There were over a dozen bodies in the main hall, including a few women and some boys who were barely in their teens. There were broken teeth and blood on the floor and walls, and a number of victims had been badly beaten. All had their hands tied behind them and there were multiple bayonet wounds on each.

I looked at Chan in disbelief. I was pretty hardened by years in Shanghai and was inured to its poverty and beggars. But I had never seen anything like this.

"Some of these are our men. Master Tu Yueh-sheng is paying five Mexican dollars a day and burial expenses to anyone who shoots at the Japs. The Japs are rounding up all Chinese and killing many on the suspicion of resisting them. We have found many scenes like this in the last week. Come, let's get out of here before they come back. We are behind Japanese lines now."

We went out the back of the building and moved in the direction of Pao Shan Road. The Pao Shan and Pao Shing Roads' area were the heart of Chapei with many shops, the Yates Girl School, the Door of Hope, the General Labor Union Headquarters, the Sikh Temple, and the Indian Youth League Headquarters. From what I could see, much of the area was in ruins or on its way there. The area had a heavy White Russian population, and I thought I could see anger and tears in Mikhail's eyes as he viewed the destruction.

That was not all that was destroyed. The safe house, which was west of Hung Shing near where it joined Pao Shan, was a casualty of the fighting. We had followed the alley that ran parallel to Hung Shing, quickly crossed Yung Shing and we were standing in the ruins of the safe house. The roof was gone and so were the people. Three walls were standing, and fortunately one of them fronted Hung Shing, sheltering us from any Japanese troops.

I realized where we were. There was the wall of a large compound in front of us and I could hear singing in Latin. It was the Vesper Service, and the wall was the back of the Holy Family Convent. And there was a door in the wall.

Holy Family had been a convent and orphanage, but now it was a school mostly for Portuguese and Chinese girls. I visited there in the past before they moved the orphanage to St. Ignatius, and I knew the Mother Superior.

"Chan, the building in front of us is the rear of a Catholic School. We can rest there. I know the nuns. When it's dark, I'm going to try the door." Chan nodded, and I prayed, really prayed, that the door was unlocked or that it would open if I pounded hard on it.

Some prayers are answered. The door was unlocked when I ran across the road an hour later, and there were two Nuns in a small garden saying the rosary. They looked up in shock at first, but one recognized me.

"Mr Ford?" Sister Mary Agnes asked. I nodded, turned, and signaled to Chan. In seconds we were all across the road, and in minutes we were in the kitchen. Food appeared, and I looked around. There were children and refugees everywhere, more than hundred. I just stared and held the chopsticks in front of my mouth.

"Eat, Mr Ford. Eat and then sleep. We are looking after your wounded friend. Sleep and we'll talk in the morning."

CHAPTER TWENTY-THREE
Wednesday-Friday, February 3-5, Holy Family Convent, Chapei

I was awakened at dawn from an exhausted sleep by a cannonade that shook the building and rolled me from my pallet to the floor. I did not know where I was at first, but I saw Sister Mary Agnes bending over two small children giving them water from a bottle and then I remembered where I was.

I felt dirty and the four days' growth of beard was starting to itch. My mouth was dry and my eyes burned. I walked over to Sister Mary Agnes and asked if there was any coffee or tea. She shook her head no.

"You are up, thank God. I am afraid we are out of just about everything. There is some water, but we are trying to conserve it for the children. The fighting has knocked out the water pipes. The little medicine we had is gone, and we are rationing the food we have. We have been trapped here since last Thursday."

I rubbed my eyes and looked around. The church was intact for the most part, but some of the stained-glass windows were broken and a stiff breeze blew through the openings. There were puddles of rain on the floor and there were people everywhere, women, a few old men, and mostly children. Many were hurt.

The temperature had to be in the thirties and people were huddled together for warmth. Most had only the clothing on their backs, the thin padded jackets the peasants wore in winter. The nuns had saved the few blankets for the babies and toddlers.

"How many are here?" I asked.

"I really don't know. There were over a hundred two days ago, but they keep arriving every time the shelling lets up. Here, take some water." She held out a bottle. I pushed it away, but she said, "You must take a little. We need your help, and I cannot afford another casualty."

"Where is Robin?"

"Your wounded friend?" she asked. "He is in the small chapel that we are using for the more seriously hurt. We changed his bandage, but the wound is infected. He will need a doctor soon. We have no antibiotics, and I worry about blood poisoning and the possibility of gangrene."

"Can you take me to him?"

"He is over there," she said pointing to an area off the nave. "I must tend to these people."

I thanked her and made my way through the bodies, some sleeping, some apparently unconscious, to the chapel off the nave. I saw Chan and Mikhail and waved them over. There was a loud boom, and I heard the whistling of shells overhead.

Mikhail was covered in dust and there was a small cut along his jaw. "We are in the middle of it, Jack," he said. "They are fighting for control of the North Station. I stuck my head out and low crawled to the wall. I think the Nationalists hold the station, but the Japanese are shelling it and the convent is in no-man's land. We are taking stray rounds from both sides."

"You're bleeding."

"Just a scratch. Some shrapnel or pieces of brick. I don't know which. It is raining down debris and lead outside. We are lucky that the church has thick walls. The area around us in ruins."

Chan joined us. "Where's your man," I asked.

"I sent him to tell Master Tu where we are."

Mikhail looked at me, then down, and then gave a small shake of the head. "At least he is a small target," Mikhail mumbled.

Robin was on a pallet at the back of the side chapel. He was sleeping, thank heaven, but there were beads of sweat on his forehead and his breath was ragged. I felt his cheeks and they were hot with fever.

A nun I did not know came over and said, "He is resting now, which is all we can do for him. We changed the bandage and cleaned the wound as best we could. But there is redness and I think it is infected. He has a fever of 103. We have very little water, but it rained a bit, and we are able to soak some rags to help cool him."

The sound of artillery was overhead, and some plaster was flaking from the ceiling. A short round or two and the roof would go.

I went back to Sister Mary Agnes. "How can we help?"

"The sisters and I can attend to the people. There is really nothing for you to do. We are running out of everything. There is some food and other items in a storage building behind the chapel, but we cannot get to it. Two men tried, but they were killed before they could get there."

"Let's take a look," I said.

The convent had several buildings besides the chapel proper where we were. There was the barracks-like building that was once the orphanage, the nun's quarters, and a series of school rooms connected by a covered walkway. I could see all this when I peered out the side door of the chapel. The storage building was against the back wall of the compound not far from the gate we had run through the night before. There were two carts leaning against the side of the storage building. And two dead bodies in the middle of the yard.

I went back and found Sister Mary Agnes. "Is the storage building locked?' I asked.

"Yes. Mother Superior has the keys."

"I think we can get to the storage building if we stay low and keep along the wall. Please ask Mother Superior for the keys."

She went off and was back in a few minutes with the Mother Superior. "I am Sister Margaret."

"Reverend Mother, I think we can retrieve some of the supplies from the storage building, but we will need the keys." She looked at me with doubt in her eyes. "We'll pick our moment, and if we stay low and close to the wall, we will be protected for most of the way. Between the three of us we should be able to load both of the carts I saw and get them back here. What is in the storage building?"

"There is rice, but that won't do us much good without water to boil it. The waterpipes were damaged the second day, and we are only getting a trickle."

"There is the old well," Sister Mary Agnes suggested. "It was the water supply before the city put in running water. It still works. We use it to get water for the garden."

"Okay," I said. "How do we get the water to the church? Is there a pipe or sluice or hose?"

"There is a cistern that has a faucet that the hose goes on."

"Where is the hose and how long is it? Will it reach the church?"

"Oh yes, we use it to water the Reverend Mother's flower beds in the summer. It's in the storage building."

"Someone will have to stay and work the pump on the well. Actually, we will need a few people to do that."

Chan said he would find volunteers. I thought to myself don't ask how he plans to get the volunteers.

The Mother Superior took a long key off a ring and handed it to me. "This is the spare key. The other key is with the men who tried earlier."

"I'll try not to lose it, "I said thinking or lose my life trying not to lose it.

———∞———

We waited until dusk before moving out. The artillery fire had lessened, but there was still the thump of the trench mortars and the whine of the bullets. The sky was thick with smoke and dust. Both sides were using flares and star shells to light the area.

There were six of us, Mikhail, Chan, the three Chinese 'volunteers' rounded up by Chan, and me. It was thirty yards from the chapel door to the wall. It was open ground, and we'd have to pick a moment between the flares to make the dash. From there, it was a low crawl to the nun's quarters and quick dash to the covered walkway of the classrooms. That would put us within thirty or forty yards of the storage building door. That thirty or forty yards was across more open ground, and the two dead bodies were a reminder that some luck would be needed.

I led the way. We all made the dash to the wall. There was some random rifle fire from the upper floor of a building that the Japanese were using as a forward observation post for their artillery spotters. We low-crawled to the nun's building, then crouched and ran to the covered walkway. A flare went up exposing the three Chinese and Mikhail who were bringing up the rear. A machine gun opened up and I saw one of the Chinese go down and Mikhail and the other two hit the dirt. Tracers cut a line a few feet above their heads. The flare went out and another was going up when Mikhail and one of the Chinese grabbed the downed man and all four made it to the nun's building and then the covered walkway.

"How bad is he?" I asked Mikhail.

"Not too bad if we can stop the bleeding. A hole in his jacket and a piece of meat off his side." Mikhail ripped part of the man's jacket and pressed it against the wound. "We'll get him on the way back." I looked Mikhail in the eye and I knew what we were both thinking, if we make it back.

I could see the storage building from the covered walk, and we were in luck. The door had been damaged by the shelling and it was hanging by one hinge. No need to fumble with the key in the open.

"I'll go and pull the door down. You follow between the flares and try to pull the carts inside."

I made the dash to the door, pulled it back, and dived inside the building. It was large, maybe 18'x12', and I could see sacks of rice and shelves with canned goods. The pump was in the middle of the room, and there was a long hose coiled beside it. I held up my palm during one of the flares to keep the others in place. I tried the pump on the well and water flowed easily. I hooked up the hose, and then went to the door to signal the others to try and cross.

They came across in twos with Chan and one of the Chinese first and then Mikhail and the other Chinese. The carts were against the side of the building away from the Japanese observation post. Chan and I crawled around to the side and quickly pulled both carts into the room. There was some rope on one of the shelves, and I tied one end of the rope to the hose and the other end to a small ax we found. It was about fifty yards in a straight line to the chapel door. I made ready to throw the ax when Mikhail grabbed my arm.

"Let me," he said. "I'm bigger and stronger." He reared back and buried the ax about a foot in front of the chapel door. "And,

I've had more practice," he said with a smile.

One of the carts was flat and we loaded six bags of rice on it. The other was more like a wheelbarrow, and we filled it with canned goods. Both were heavy but manageable. It had started to rain again and the ground was turning to mud. Chan and I pulled the door off the hinges and laid it flat on the ground. We pulled three of the shelves free and pushed them out on top of the door. I slid out on my belly and laid the shelves end to end until we'd covered the thirty some yards between the storage room and the covered walkway.

It started to rain harder as I finished putting down the shelves, and that was the luck and cover we needed. We left two men to man the pump. I grabbed the wheelbarrow, and Mikhail and Chan each grabbed a handle of the cart, which must have weighed over 200 pounds with the rice. We made our way to the covered walkway.

I pulled up the planks and we moved to the end of the walkway. The wounded Chinese was lying on his side, and he was in shock. I started toward him, but Chan pulled me back and both Chan and Mikhail were slowly shaking their heads. He wasn't going to make it.

The rain was coming down very hard now, and it was hard to see but it would be hard to see us too. We couldn't low crawl to the wall with the carts. We'd have to make a dash from the gap where the walkway met the nun's quarters to the chapel door. I pushed one shelf, then another, and then the last one out ahead, but we were still nine yards short of the chapel door and ground was turning muddier by the second. I went into the school room, opened a storage cabinet, and broke out three more shelves. I slid them forward by lying on my stomach.

Chan and Michael went first. The shelves sank into the mud a bit, but they were able to get the cart to the door and dump the contents on the chapel floor. They pushed the cart aside and pulled the bags of rice out of the doorway. I dashed low with the wheelbarrow of canned goods and spilled the contents through the door and onto the floor of the chapel. I left the wheelbarrow by the door and grabbed the ax.

Chan, Mikhail, and I pulled the rope and in a few minutes we had about six feet of hose inside the chapel. Chan signaled with a flashlight to the two men in the storage building to start pumping. In minutes we were filling basins, tubs, and anything else that could hold water. The nuns organized a bucket brigade, and we moved the water to the cooking area and the side chapel where the sick and wounded were. After forty minutes, we signaled the two men to stop pumping.

Sister Mary Agnes and the Mother Superior were waiting for us by the door and helped organize the bucket brigade and the movement of the rice and canned goods to the cooking area. I handed the key back to the Mother Superior.

"I didn't need it," I said. "Providence stepped in."

"God stepped in," she said firmly, "and the Blessed Virgin. We prayed hard for your success and safety. Did the three Chinese men stay at the well?"

"Just two," I said. "One was killed."

"Oh. We will pray for him." She made the sign of the cross. "God has given us a small miracle. Please rest. Let me have your wet things and we will clean them. God bless you."

We were all soaked and shaking from the cold and rain. The nuns brought us some blankets, and I quickly feel asleep from the exertion and the faded adrenalin rush.

———∽∾∽———

The next day is more a series of impressions. Vivid moments caught as if in a flashbulb rather than distinct memories. With one exception, the miracle at dusk on the fifth.

The fighting around the North Station was intense now. Shells and small arms fire were hitting all around us, and pieces of the church roof were coming down. The nuns were moving from place to place within the chapel, comforting children, passing out food and water, which was still tightly rationed. You slept where you could, but the air was so thick with dust and plaster and smoke that your eyes burned and your ears rang from the shelling. It seemed to be on top of us. I thought this must be what the Somme was like during the artillery barrages in The Great War.

Fear was palpable. Hands shook and voices were hoarse and strained trying to be heard above the din. The small children were quiet, too afraid and too tired to do anything but cling to a parent, if they had one, a nun, or one another. The babies just cried.

Chan, Mikhail, and I helped wherever and however we could. We considered another run to the storage building, but the fighting was too intense. The buildings to our south near the North Train Station burned like a funeral pyre. It had to be the Commercial Press complex and its Oriental Library. I thought about Connie and how she must feel.

There didn't seem to be any pattern that I could see to the firing. Orange-red muzzle flashes of the Japanese artillery cut the night and filled the air with the pungent smell of nitroglycerin, sawdust, and graphite. The Nationalists answered back from their positions. The idea seemed to be to just pour down as much lead as possible and destroy everything. We could hear aircraft overhead and they strafed the convent yard a few times.

This went on for two days, and supplies were starting to run low again. To make matters worse the hose from the well was cut by a shell or the strafing because the water stopped. I don't think

I've ever been that thirsty, and the nuns were doing their best to see that everyone got some but took almost none for themselves. People just huddled together, too afraid to move, and shook with each explosion.

Ash filtered down through the holes in the roof and settled on your skin. It was in your hair and mouth. If you scratched, you bled and it was in your blood. The rain had stopped during the night and there was nothing to clean the air. An explosion at the base of the east wall of the church brought down a section of it, and a portion of the roof fell with it burying some of the refugees.

Chan, Mikhail, the nuns, and I pulled at the bricks and freed a number of people. Some had broken bones and a small girl had an ear hanging loose. A nun scooped her up and wrapped some cloth around her head. Mikhail, Chan, and I tried to stack some of rubble to provide some cover from the rounds that were coming through the opening but had to stop. The firing was too intense. So, we herded people to safer areas in the chapel. Some just stood there unable to move until we gently pushed them.

And then the shelling stopped. Just stopped. The light was fading. It was dusk. And the church door opened, and there was a tall figure in a white cassock standing there backlit by the flames from the burning buildings around us. I just stared not believing it. Father Jacquinot.

CHAPTER TWENTY-FOUR
Friday Night Early Saturday Morning
February 5-6 Holy Family Convent, Chapei

"How?" was all I could think of to say.

"Not now, Jack. We'll talk later. There is much to do. We need to prepare these people to leave in the morning."

"But."

"Not now, Fu Fei. Just like 1927 all over again, huh?" he said with a smile that was reassuring somehow. "Except for the Japanese and the amount of lead in the air, of course." He went off, gathering the nuns around him and giving orders. His calm seemed to reassure others, even the Chinese who had never seen or heard of Old Do Things.

It was night now and the light from the fires lit the inside of the church and cast shadows on the walls. The fighting had died down a bit, but there were the star shells and flares that brightened the night and illuminated soldiers at their positions. You could see the fallen in the streets. They seemed to be mostly Chinese and civilians by their dress. And when the wind blew in from the east, it brought the smell of corruption and flies and vermin. That smell is something that will never leave me.

Before Father Jacquinot arrived, we were all just frozen

in place. Even the children had become quiet, either dead or too tired or frightened to cry. But now the nuns were moving about, and Father Jacquinot was giving orders. He seemed to be everywhere. Cajoling, triaging the refugees, separating the dead and the too weak to move, bundling people into small groups, appointing a leader for each group, and comforting, reassuring, scolding when necessary, and ministering. His deep bass voice, commanding yet calming, "Deinde, ego te absolve a peccatis tuis in nominee Patris et Filii et Spiritus Sancti. Amen." It came back to me from my days in the Catholic orphanage in California: I absolve you of all your sins in the name of the Father, Son, and Holy Spirit.

The nuns were bending over people, pressing a rosary in their hands or stroking their foreheads. Some were tearing strips of cloth, wetting them, and tying them as masks over noses and mouths to keep the dust out and the smells at bay. Father Jacquinot, Chan, Michael, and I prepared litters for the wounded, ill, and aged who could not walk. We put Robin on the flat cart from the storage building.

It was 3:00 a.m. or so when Father Jacquinot sat down beside me in one of the pews. "I have done about all that can be done at this point, except keep praying. Tu, or I should say, one of Tu's lieutenants, told me you might be here." He smiled. "Still, a bit of a surprise but a nice one. I'll need your help and the help of your two friends to get these people across Boundary Road, Soochow Creek, and to safety in the International Settlement."

I was still not believing it. "How...?" I asked.

"How what? How did I get here? How are we going to get out?" he paused and added, "alive?"

"Yes, just how everything. We found Robin. He's hurt but here. How is Connie? What has happened...?"

He held up his hand. "One thing at a time. You left Shanghai on Thursday, right? Well, that is when the fighting broke out." He pulled a small flask from inside his cassock took a sip and passed it to me. Brandy. It was good. "Prayer is powerful and wonderful, but sometimes I need something of a different spiritual nature to fortify my aging temporal body." He smiled again and began to talk.

"The Japs have bitten off more than they can chew at the moment. The 19th Route Army is putting up a hell of a resistance and inflicting heavy casualties on Shiozawa's marines. Tokyo is unhappy and has kicked Shiozawa upstairs and replaced him with General Ueda. The fighting is messy, Jack. There are no clear front lines. A salient here and there and it's impossible to tell who controls what. Some of the hardest fighting is around here at the North Train Station. The 19th brought in an armored train with heavy artillery and the station has changed hands a couple of times.

"The Japanese have become more brutal as the fighting has gotten harder. Chinese snipers are taking their toll from destroyed buildings and side streets. The Japs are rounding up and executing on the spot anyone they suspect of helping the Nationalists, and they suspect everyone. In a couple of instances, they have even pushed Chinese civilians ahead of them when they have encountered Nationalist strong points. You've seen the damage the artillery has done to Chapei, both Nationalist and Japanese. And the Japs have set fire to buildings in an effort to burn out the snipers.

"The SVC has tried to keep the Japanese from shelling Nationalist positions from inside the Settlement. Your 4th Marines hold Sector C just across from us. They chased some Japanese troops out of their sector two days ago. But the Japanese have pushed into the Western Roads around Jessfield. They are strafing the refugee camps. They are reorganizing their forces ahead of another push against the 19th."

"We thought about trying to get through at Jessfield," I said, "but heard the Japanese were planning to attack there, so we came in from the north. Chan said the Green Gang had safe house near here, but when we got there, it had been destroyed. I recognized The Holy Family Convent, and we were able to take shelter here. But how did you get here? It's a miracle."

"Connie got the cable you sent from Peking, and she told me that you had found Robin. Then I was visited two days ago by a man who I knew to have ties to Tu and the Green Gang. He said you were headed for a safe house in Chapei. It's lucky you were able to take shelter here, such as it is."

"How is Connie?"

"She is safe. The fighting has stayed out of the International Settlement for the most part and the old Chinese City, for that matter. The Japanese have launched attacks from the areas of the Settlement they control north of Soochow Creek, but the Nationalists have been careful not to fire on Japanese positions in the Settlement. It is amazing the way the Chinese have rallied to support the 19th Route Army, Jack. Women and children even are carrying water to the troops and caring for the wounded. The Japanese have awakened the Chinese giant."

"How did you get here, though? The shelling and fighting have been awful."

"I went to Chin Te-li and told him I need his help in evacuating the civilians from the Convent. He told me the British and the Americans were trying to arrange a ceasefire, but the Japanese weren't having any of it. He said he would ask General Tsai to cease artillery attacks and offensive operations long enough for me to get here and then get everyone back across the Creek. I told him I needed an hour to get here and two hours to get everyone out. I then saw Tachibana and asked him to intercede with the

Japanese high command. He agreed. The Japanese needed a lull anyway, so Ueda can reorganize his troops, and their main push was toward Woosung anyway. So, I got here.

"We leave here at 10:00 a.m. today," he said. "I'll lead from the front, and I want you and your two friends to bring up the rear. We only have a couple of hours to get everyone across and we need to keep them together and moving. I'm pretty sure the Nationalists will honor their word. I'm less sure about the Japanese, but I stressed to Tachibana that the last thing Japan needed was to kill a Jesuit priest leading orphans out of a combat zone. The press has been hard on Japan, and the Brits and Yanks are raising holy hell in the diplomatic circles. So, let's just pray we'll be okay. Oh, and by the way, in case you haven't noticed, today is the Lunar New Year. The Year of the Monkey. Lots of fun ahead don't you think." He winked.

CHAPTER TWENTY-FIVE
Saturday, February 6,
Holy Family Convent, Chapei

Father Jacquinot had organized the evacuees in groups of ten with a leader for each one. It was a take-off on the old Chinese pao-chia system that they all knew. At dawn he called all the pao-chia leaders and nuns together to brief us on what he planned to do.

"We leave at 10:00 a.m. sharp. I will be in front with the Mother Superior. I will be holding high the silver crucifix from the altar and the Reverend Mother will have the statute of the Blessed Virgin. Each leader is responsible for his ten people. You are to stay in line and to keep pace. The children will be in the middle along with the sick and the litters. The Sisters will walk on the outside edge of our formation. Mr Ford and his colleagues will bring up the rear. We will be a moving box. It is imperative that we all stay together. There can be no stragglers."

Father Jacquinot paused and then repeated it all in Shanghai dialect. He asked if everyone understood. We all nodded our heads.

"Okay, this is the line of march. Out the front of the Church down North Honan Road. We cross Boundary Road and we are in the International Settlement. But the Japanese control that area so we are still not safe. We turn on right on Haining Road, cross North Chekiang Road, and turn left and south on North Thibet Road. We cross Soochow Creek on the Markham Bridge. This is the sector held by the US 4th Marines. They know we are coming and they will protect us. The Marines have trucks and vehicles for us. The refugees will go to the old Chinese City where you will be provided for. The sick and wounded will be taken to Lester Hospital. Are there any questions?"

There were none. "You all know your places in the formation. Get your people ready now. Jack and your team, please stay with me." The nuns and pao-chia leaders went off to organize their groups.

"Jack, I don't know what we will run into. The distance isn't great, just a mile or so, but we will be walking through the middle of a war zone. Pray, and I am serious about this, pray that both sides hold fire. If there are shots, keep the people moving. We cannot allow the group to scatter. It will cause one side or the other to open fire. The column will almost certainly string out. We need to be prepared for that, and Jack, your team must do all you can to keep the people moving. If people fall or can't keep up, we'll have to leave them behind or have one of the men in a pao-chia put them on their back. I will send the Reverend Mother across the Markham Bridge with the refugees. I'll stay on this side helping to keep the flow moving and then we'll all cross together. I talked to your friend, Captain Bowman. He says the Marines are under strict orders to stay on their side of Soochow Creek. So, we are on our own until we cross the bridge."

Chan, Mikhail, and I huddled and discussed how we would operate. I put Chan on the left flank of the column and Mikhail on the right. Chan's two volunteers would be in front of us pushing the rear ranks of the column forward.

Mikhail said, "We need something to designate the end of the column. We have the crucifix and statute of the Virgin at the front, but we need something for the back."

"You're right," I said. I looked around and said, "We'll use that," and pointed at the large yellow and white Vatican flag that stood near the altar. "I'll carry it and walk a few paces behind the column."

I went to the side chapel to check on Robin. He was conscious and was on the cart from the storage building along with two elderly Chinese women. I told him what we planned and he just nodded. His face was flushed and his forehead was hot. Fever. There was a strong, putrid smell too. I couldn't tell if it was from Robin's wound or from one of the others. I walked to a corner of the chapel, knelt, and said a prayer.

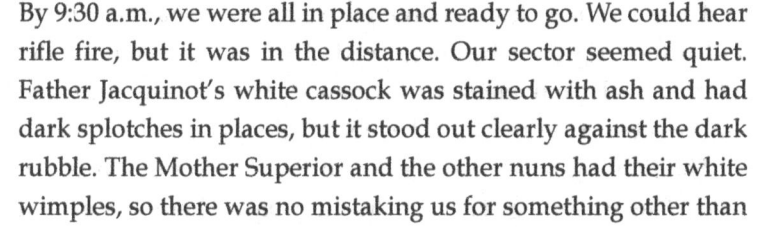

By 9:30 a.m., we were all in place and ready to go. We could hear rifle fire, but it was in the distance. Our sector seemed quiet. Father Jacquinot's white cassock was stained with ash and had dark splotches in places, but it stood out clearly against the dark rubble. The Mother Superior and the other nuns had their white wimples, so there was no mistaking us for something other than the religious evacuation Father Jacquinot had promised both sides.

At 10:00 a.m. sharp, Father Jacquinot threw open the doors of the church and marched out boldly holding high the silver crucifix. No gunfire. He was singing Onward Christian Soldiers at the top of his lungs, and the nuns were fingering rosaries and saying Hail Marys. The Mother Superior had the statue of the Virgin Mary in her arms. There had to be over three hundred of us, and it took most of a half hour before my team exited, bringing up the rear. I could see the silver crucifix ahead of us.

CITY OF LOST SOULS

When I got a good look at North Honan Road in the daylight, I was stunned by the extent of the destruction. All the landmarks were gone, the shops and theaters and restaurants, all of them pitted with bullet holes. Walls caved in, tattered signs, and smoldering ashes. We maneuvered around the broken masonry in the road. The formulation was holding together pretty well. There was some stringing out, but people were keeping pace for the most part. The stretcher bearers and men pushing the carts were doing well. People were helping one another.

Shots rang out periodically and we all ducked reflexively but the shots were not at us. Both sides were abiding by their agreement with Father Jacquinot. There had been no effort to clean up the dead. Civilian and military lay where they fell, and the smell was awful. The rags some of us had tied around our mouths and noses did little to keep the odor out. The scavengers were out. I saw a dog with a small human hand in its mouth.

There was less destruction after we crossed Boundary Road and turned right on Haining Road. This was the edge of the International Settlement and Chapei. There were Japanese sentries at every corner, but they left us alone.

The fighting was a few blocks north and west of where we were. This was a rear area for the most part. There was even a company of Shanghai firefighters trying to keep the blazes from spreading farther into the International Settlement. They just stood gaping at us as we went by.

We were strung out more than we wanted to be at this point. The two Chinese volunteers were encouraging the refugees to speed up and close up. The nuns on the sides of the column were doing the same. Some of the older, weaker refugees and children were beginning to falter. I saw the nuns pick up children and put them on their shoulders.

The column turned left on North Thibet Road, and the

Markham Bridge and safety was just two blocks ahead. I could see the silver crucifix Father Jacquinot held stationary and above the heads of the refugees. The column picked up speed, now seeing the bridge and safety.

Father Jacquinot walked back to where we were. There were only about forty more people to get across. "Robin is across, Jack. I saw him into an ambulance. He should be at Lester Hospital in a few minutes."

"Thank you, Father. I can't thank you enough. I don't know what we would have done without you. I'll always remember you walking out of the chaos and into that church."

They were on us before we realized it. Six or seven ronin, pistols out and firing. Tanaka's men had probably shadowed us from the convent, awaiting their chance. One of Chan's volunteers went down, and the remaining refugees ran for the bridge, pushing and shoving some of the slower and weaker ones into Soochow Creek. A bullet whipped by me and another ricocheted off the crucifix, which spun out of Father Jacquinot's hand.

Mikhail had his pistol out as did Chan. They were firing at the ronin. One went down and then another. I saw one rush Father Jacquinot and the big Webley came out of his cassock and he swung it against the side of the man's head. He went down with a thud.

I dropped the flag and pushed Father Jacquinot to the ground. A ronin was coming at us with a samurai sword. The scene just freezes in my mind. The sword coming up readying to strike. The .45 in my hand, and then a huge hole in the ronin's chest as he was blown backward by the blast.

One tossed a Type 91 grenade and I saw Mikhail pick it up to throw it back. But it went off and Mikhail's torso took the full effect of the blast. Chan stepped forward and put two rounds into the head of the ronin who lobbed it.

Then it was over. Four dead ronin, the others running off. Father Jacquinot down on the ground unhurt. I was unscathed. Chan and one volunteer were okay. One volunteer and Mikhail dead. The butcher's bill.

"He saved our lives," Chan said. "He could have kicked it away or used that one," pointing at the dead volunteer, "as a shield, but he didn't. And we are alive. We are alive." Chan just shook his head. Don't let anyone tell you the Chinese are stoic about death or that Asians think life is cheap.

We crossed the bridge and Phil Bowman was there. "We were about to open fire on those bastards, but it was over too quick," he said. "Are you okay, Jack? We pulled the refugees out of the creek and the guy on the cart is on his way to Lester Hospital in an ambulance. I have a Navy Corpsman riding with him."

"I'm okay. We have two dead, a Chinese and a White Russian, who were helping us. Can you take charge of the bodies until we make arrangements? It'll only be for a day or two. I just need to…"

"We got it, Jack. Don't worry. I have a car. We'll take you to your flat. Father Jacquinot is accompanying the refugees to the Chinese City. Making sure that they are taken care of. Come along. Let's get out of here."

Connie was at the flat waiting for me. Lao Wu opened the door and Connie threw her arms around me and kissed me hard.

"We got Robin," I said. "He is hurt but he'll be okay. He's in Lester Hospital."

She hugged me tighter and kissed me gently. "Later Jack. Tell me all about it later. Now, a bath and bed."

I pulled away for a second and walked over to Saudade, who

was bobbing up and down wildly and screaming at the top of her voice "he lo he lo he lo he lo". I gave her a piece of melon, and she bobbed a bit more. Connie took me by the hand and led to the bedroom and bath at the back of the flat.

CHAPTER TWENTY-SIX
Sunday, Monday February 7-8

The weak winter sun was through the bedroom window when I woke the next morning. Connie was already awake when I opened my eyes. She just smiled at me.

"I let you sleep. You were exhausted. You almost feel asleep in the tub." Connie was laying on her side, her head supported by her right palm. "Lie here with me for a bit. We'll go see Robin this afternoon." She nuzzled close to me and put her arm over my chest.

"How was it? Getting back, I mean. I was very worried when Father Jacquinot told me how you were getting here."

"It was difficult. We really had no choice. The Japanese were hunting us in Peking, and we couldn't fly or take the train. And they almost got us at the bridge. Mikhail is dead." There was a sharp intake of breath from Connie. "He saved us really. He and Chan. Chan is Green Gang. Big Ears Tu sent him to Peking with Mikhail. Chan found Robin and managed our escape."

"How did Mikhail die?"

"At the bridge when the ronin jumped us. He put himself between a Jap grenade and us. And...and, I killed one of them.

Shot him." I rolled on my side and held her close to me.

"Wellington Chu is dead, too," she said. "He tried to protect the Oriental Library and he died in the fire. The Japanese set fire to the library, Jack." She pushed back from me and sat upright in the bed. "They set fire to it on purpose. I saw it with Carl Crow from the roof of the Park Hotel. We were on their terrace watching the fighting and I saw it burn. All those priceless books and objects destroyed. And all my father's work. His life's work. Mine too, I guess."

She began to cry. Heavy sobs, her shoulders shaking. I pulled her down and held her close again.

"Not everything. Robin has the special items your father left with Ding Mu. We'll get them when we see Robin." I felt her head nod against my shoulder, and I held her until she cried herself out.

———∞———

We looked in on Robin that afternoon. He was conscious and his fever had broken. The antibiotics were fighting the infection, but the wound was more serious than we thought. The bullet had gone through and missed the bone but tore up muscle and connective tissue. The infection had done more damage. His right arm would always be weak and of limited use.

His spirits were good, though. I left Connie there with him and went to Aurora University to find Father Jacquinot. He was in his office, his small desk covered with stacks of paper. He looked up and said, "Come in, Jack. Come in. How are you? Have you seen Robin? How is he?"

"I've just come from Lester Hospital. Connie is with him, and they are catching up. He is mending. It will be slow, I think, and he will only have partial use of his right arm. But he'll live. How are the refugees and the nuns?'

"The sisters are at St. Ignatius, and they are fine. The refugees are all crowded into the old Chinese city. It's tough there, but they are safe, and tough is nothing new for them. I'm trying to arrange aid. That is what all this paper is about." He waved his good arm at the mess on the desk. "The clergy are banding together with the SMC to provide longer-term relief. We'll be able to do it."

"Robin found Ding Mu and brought back the scrolls Baker-Kerr left with him. Connie has them. So not a complete loss."

"How is she? I was on the roof terrace of the Park Hotel when the Japanese set fire to the library. They tried to blame it on the Nationalists, but they did it. First the shelling and then burning the buildings to keep snipers from using them."

"She is taking it hard. The British reserve is in place, but I know her well enough now that I can see through it. Oh, before I forget, please thank imam Ma. We never would have found Robin without his help. And I need to thank Tu, too. He may be a gangster, but we would not have found Robin, or be alive, if not for the Green Gang's help. He's quite the Chinese patriot. Many of the snipers are his and he pays them to kill Japs."

"I know about Tu. He's had a falling out with his partners in crime among the French officials here. He is ruthless but right now he is ruthless for us. And I should thank you, Jack, really. That shove you gave me probably saved me from being badly hurt if not killed."

"I can still see it if I close my eyes. I try not think about it."

"Prayer and confession are powerful things, Jack. All that is required is to use them."

Mikhail's funeral service was Monday at St. Nicholas Russian Orthodox Church in Frenchtown. Connie, Chan, and Father

Jacquinot went with me, and the cream of the White Russian diaspora turned out in all its old splendor. Czarist uniforms were the order of the day and ladies in long black mourning clothes. Gold braid and epaulets, doubled-breasted tunics with medals, and sashes with court honors were all on display.

Mikhail Andreyevich Petrov lay in a beautiful open teak casket provided by Tu Yueh-sheng. Mikhail was dressed in white according to Orthodox tradition, and as the mourners circled the casket, we placed flowers inside. The service was in Russian and moving even though I could not understand a word of. I did recognize Psalm 118 and followed along in the Bible Connie had brought: "Oh, give thanks to the Lord for He is good! For His mercy endures forever." The service ended with the priest anointing Mikhail with oil and pulling the funeral shroud up over him.

He was laid to his final rest in the Bubbling Well Road Cemetery. Mourners took a handful of dirt and tossed it in the grave. There was a reception after at the Russian Ex-Officers' Club on Rue Corneille. Many toasts and some tears and some laughs, too.

Connie, Father Jacquinot, and I went to dinner at the Cercle Sportif Francais. Then Connie and I went back to my flat, opened a good bottle of wine, and held hands on the loveseat in the living room. Too much sadness over too many sad days to say anything. We were each alone in our thoughts.

CHAPTER TWENTY-SEVEN
March 1932

The fighting continued through the first two weeks of March when a truce was signed and negotiations on an armistice started. It was the beginning of the end for Shanghai, the Shanghai I knew, anyway. The militarists continued to nibble at China until August 1937, when they staged another incident, this time outside Peking, and launched an all-out invasion. The International Settlement and the French Concession were safe, but Chapei and the area around Shanghai were devastated again. Crime and general lawlessness plagued the Extra Roads area, and ronin and Chinese thugs in their pay carried out bombings and assassinations. The Nationalists retaliated as best they could while retreating into the interior.

But that was still five years away. Shanghai continued to dance and pretend the "War at the End of the Street" hadn't happened or didn't matter. The Shanghai Race Club held its spring meet with Mister Cinders winning the Champions' Stake. The night life continued as before, perhaps a bit more frenzied, if only because we were all looking over our shoulders wondering what Japan would do next. The trading houses made money even in the Great Depression. And refugees continued to flow into the city.

I had one bit of unfinished business. I talked to Phil Bowman, Mike Finley, and Father Jacquinot, and then I asked Phil to invite Tachibana to drinks at the American Club on Foochow Road. When he walked in, Phil greeted him and escorted him to a private room at the back of the building. I was already there, and with me were Finley, Father Jacquinot, Chan, and two of Mikhail's White Russian friends.

"Welcome, Tachibana-san. Sit down please. Phil, please pour our guest a whisky." He looked surprised for a moment but quickly regained his composure. "I have a message for you and for Major Tanaka and anyone else associated with the ronin. My friends are here because this is their message too, and they want to see it delivered." He showed no emotion or reaction.

"I believe you had a role in the death of Sydney Baker-Kerr and in the attacks on his son Robert in Peking and on me and Father Jacquinot and Chan at the Markham Bridge. They stop now. If I as much as see you or a ronin anywhere near me or the Baker-Kerrs, I will shoot to kill. Mr Finley of Special Branch, Captain Bowman, Father Jacquinot, and Mr Chan, who is a close associate of Mr Tu Yueh-sheng, will hunt you down if anything happens to me or the Baker-Kerrs. These two Russian gentlemen were close friends of Mikhail Petrov, who died at Markham Bridge. They would like nothing more than an excuse to open fire on anyone they believe is in any way connected to the murder of their fellow officer. It is a matter of honor to them, something I know the Japanese officer corps understands very well. And do tell Major Tanaka our business is not over should I ever see him again. You may leave."

He stood, still showing no emotion, and Phil led him to the door. He hadn't touched the whisky, and I threw the glass and its contents against the wall where it shattered.

"You know, Jack," Phil said," you're the first person I want as a friend and the last person I want as an enemy."

Connie and I continued to see a great deal of one another. We did the town, had dinner with friends, and helped Robin with his recovery. But I could see the great pain she felt, and the way events were weighing on her. So, I was not surprised when she told me she and Robin were leaving. We were having drinks in the Horse and Hounds Bar.

"Jack, there's no other way to say this...but Robin and I are leaving Shanghai. There are too many bad memories here." She smiled, "And some very good ones, but I can never be happy here or feel safe." There were tears in her eyes.

I held her hand. "I understand. I think I even saw this moment coming. When are you leaving? Going back to England?"

"No, there is nothing in England for us. We're going to Singapore. We should be safe there. Victor Sassoon has given Robin a letter of introduction that he can use to land a position with one of the trading companies there or in Bombay or Calcutta. We leave tomorrow on the P&O liner. I thought it better to wait to tell you. Less time for regret." She gave a little half laugh.

"Yes, you are probably doing the right thing."

"Come with us. Not right away, of course, but soon."

"I can't, Connie. This is the only home I've known and there is nothing for me in Singapore or India. Too old, too settled to start over. A last night on the town? A pleasant memory to leave with? For both of us."

"Yes, I'd like that," and she wiped her right eye.

We had dinner in the Tower Restaurant, and then hit the clubs in Frenchtown. We saw Whitey Smith and Buck Clayton and finished the night at the Del Monte. We danced our last dance to Cole Porter's "Night and Day." "Night and day, you are the one. Only you beneath the moon and under the sun."

I drove her back to the Villa Apartments, where she had been living with Robin since his release from the hospital. I rode up in the elevator and we paused by the door.

"Do you want to come in? Robin is asleep."

I shook my head, "No, I think it is better if I go." She kissed me lightly on the lips like the first time by the elevator in the Cathay.

"I'll send Peter with the car to take you to the jetty."

———∞———

I drove the Packard to the Missions Building and parked. It was a sunny day, and the temperature was in the upper forties. You could believe that spring was not far away. I walked to the jetty and was standing there when Peter dropped them off. I shook Robin's hand, and he thanked me for all I had done.

Connie said she had a small gift for me. It was an art deco Ronson Fine Line cigar lighter inscribed with J, the Chinese character for love, and C. If you change the tone from falling to rising, "ai" changes its meaning from "to love" to "to suffer." I shook my head a little and thanked her.

Connie took my hand and said, "Please think about Singapore."

I watched them walk up the gangplank. I heard the klaxon sound and the weighing of the anchor. I watched the tugs push the liner out into the channel and start it up the Whangpoo to the Yangtze and the sea. The city, which always seemed lonely to me, was lonelier. I drove the Packard to St. Ignatius, and I went inside. I sat in a back pew for a while thinking woulda, coulda, and shoulda before driving home to the Blackstone where Lao Wu would have dinner and Saudade waited.

CITY OF LOST SOULS

I never saw her again.

August 1971 California
"Hello, Mr Ford. It's me, the PhD candidate at Berkeley. You said I should call you back about wanting to talk about Shanghai in 1932."
"Yes. I'm sorry. I really would like to help you, but I can't. I just don't have many memories from that period. I'm sure others can help you, though. Good luck with your dissertation. I'm sure you'll do very well without me. Most people do."

Notes on People and Places

All the places mentioned in City of Lost Souls actually existed, and I've tried to be true to their character and appearance. Many of the people Jack encounters are real, but their interactions with Jack and one another are, of course, total fiction and a product of my imagination. The events and chronology of the 1932 fighting are accurate.

Father Robert Jacquinot de Besange, S.J. was a truly remarkable man. The 1932 rescue of the Holy Family Convent is entirely fictional but based on the actual one that he pulled off in 1927 during Chiang's coup against the left-wing Nationalists and their communist allies. He was very popular.

He did lose a hand making fireworks and he did teach at Aurora. He was the Chaplain of the Shanghai Volunteer Corps. He helped establish the National Flood Relief Commission to aid the victims of the 1931 floods. During the 1937 fighting, he created the Jacquinot Safe Zone in the old Chinese City to shelter refugees. This was a model for the one established by the German Rabe in Nanking during the Rape of Nanking. Father Jacquinot continued to work on behalf of Chinese refugees until he left Shanghai and China in June 1940. He continued to work on refugee and displaced person issues after World War II. He died in 1946. Marcia Ristaino tells his story in *The Jacquinot Safe Zone*.

Sir Aurel Stein was a British archeologist, who led four expeditions to Central Asia between 1906 and 1930. During the 1906-1907 expedition, he discovered the "Caves of the Thousand Buddhas" near Dunhuang, China. Among the discoveries was a printed copy of the Diamond Sutra, which dated from 868 AD and is regarded as the world's oldest printed text. He brought back more than 40,000 scrolls.

Count Kozui Otani backed three expeditions to the same general area as Stein from 1902-1910. The 1910 expedition included **Zuicho Tachibana**, a Japanese Naval Officer, and Elizaburo Nomura, an Imperial Army Officer. They traveled as Priests of the Pure Land Buddhist Sect, but the British thought they were spies. Peter Hopkirk's *Foreign Devils on the Silk Road* is a lively account of these expeditions. The **Kaifeng Jews** have existed in China since at least the Northern Song dynasty (960-1127). Kaifeng was the capital of the Northern Song and was a major city on the Silk Road.

Carl Crow, Stirling Fessenden, John Powell, and Carroll Alcott were all prominent Americans in Shanghai. Carl Crow ran a major advertising agency in Shanghai and was a vocal supporter of the Chinese people. He wrote several books, including guidebooks, about China.

Stirling Fessenden was a lawyer and served as Chairman of the Shanghai Municipal Council from 1923-1929 and Secretary-General of the Council from 1929 to 1939. **Carroll Alcott** was a newspaperman and radio broadcaster, and he was sharply critical of Japan, which threatened his life and tried to jam his radio broadcasts over XMHA. **John Powell** was the publisher and editor of the *China Weekly Review*, and, like Carroll and Crow, was a strong supporter of China and critical of the Japanese. Crow and Alcott left Shanghai before Pearl Harbor and escaped Japanese retribution. Fessenden and Powell were not so fortunate. Fessenden died in Shanghai in 1944 after refusing repatriation. He was ill and gave his slot up so that someone else could leave. Powell was arrested, tortured, and crippled before being repatriated in 1943. Alcott and Powell wrote about their experiences: Alcott's *My War with Japan* and Powell's *My Twenty-Five Years in China*.

Tu Yueh-sheng and **Pock-marked Huang** were leaders of the Green Gang, a triad that controlled the opium traffic in Shanghai and was active in many other criminal activities. Tu was a strong supporter of Chiang Kai-shek, and actively supported his 1927 coup against the left wing of the Nationalists and their communist allies. Tu did pay snipers in the 1932 fighting—five Mexican dollars a day and burial if killed. During WWII, Tu was in Chungking, and the Green Gang supported the Nationalist espionage head in sabotage and intelligence collection operations against the Japanese. Tu fled to Hong Kong when the communists took over in 1949 and he died there.

Huang, who owned the Great World Amusement Center, was the Chief of Chinese Detectives of the very corrupt French Police. After the Communist takeover in 1949, Huang stayed on and succumbed to his opium addiction. Pan Lin's *Old Shanghai Gangsters in Paradise* recounts Tu's and Huang's story. Josef Von Sternberg left a very funny description of the Great World in his book *Fun in a Chinese Laundry*.

Etienne Fiori, a Corsican and a member of the Union Corse, was Chief of Police in the French Concession. In 1933 the French Consul General and Fiori cracked down on the Green Gang in an effort to clean up the concession and repair the poor reputation of the French administration. Tu got his revenge. He invited the French Consul General and Fiori to dinner and poisoned them. The Consul General died, but Fiori survived and left Shanghai.

Sir Ellice Victor Sassoon was British and educated at Harrow and Trinity College, Cambridge, but his family was originally from Baghdad. They immigrated to British India and made their money there. In the 1920s, Sassoon moved his business interests to Shanghai and was one of the drivers of the real estate boom. He built the Cathay Hotel on the Bund, the best in Shanghai and one of the finest in the world. He was known for his lavish parties, devotion to the races, and love of the ladies. He moved his interests to the Bahamas after the communists took over. *Shanghai Grand* by Taras Grescoe is the story of Sassoon's Shanghai days.

Ryukichi Tanaka was a Japanese intelligence officer operating in China and Shanghai in the late 1920s and early 1930s. In his memoirs, he claimed responsibility for staging the 1932 incident with the Buddhist monks that was the pretext for the Japanese attacks. He had a mistress who was a Manchu princess and close to Puyi, the last emperor of China and later puppet emperor of Manchukuo. She was quite a colorful character in her own right, dressing as a man at times and running part of Tanaka's espionage operation. Her Manchu name translated as **Eastern Jewel** but she went by **Yoshiko Kawashima**. She was captured by the Nationalists after war and executed for treason. Tanaka became a Major General and Commandant of the primary espionage and training academy for the Japanese army.

Daisetu Suzuki was a Zen Buddhist scholar and defender of Japanese militarism. The views expressed to Father Jacquinot by Tachibana and attributed to Suzuki are accurate.

The **US 4th Marines** were sent to Shanghai in January 1927 to protect American interests. They left Shanghai for the Philippines in late November 1941. They were part of the defense of Bataan and Corregidor, and the survivors became Japanese prisoners of war. *Hold High the Torch* by Condit and Turnbladh is a history of the 4th Marines. The **19th Route Army** was one of the Nationalists' best units. It acquitted itself very well in both the 1932 and the 1937 fighting with the Japanese. *China's Trail by Fire* by Donald Jordan is a detailed account of the 1932 fighting.

The various British officials mentioned in specific positions occupied those positions in 1932. **Roger Hollis**, later knighted, worked for the British American Tobacco Company in Shanghai and Peking. He may or may not have been an intelligence officer at the time, but he was definitely a member of MI-5 by 1938. He served as Director-General of MI-5 from 1956-1965.

The various personalities peppered through the book (**Whitey Smith, Buck Clayton, Joe and Nellie Farren, Demon Hyde, Al Israel, Jimmy James, and Jack Riley among others**) are real people. Whitey Smith wrote a book about his experiences, *I Didn't Make a Million*. Paul French chronicles the doings of some of the more notorious members of this group, like the Farrens and Jack Riley, in his book *City of Devils*.

The **madams** mentioned in the book are real and ran high-end brothels.

Saudade: a feeling of longing, melancholy, or nostalgia that is supposedly characteristic of the Portuguese or Brazilian temperament.

Note on Chinese Names, Places, and People

Although pinyin has been the most commonly used system for romanizing Chinese names since the 1980s, I have chosen to use the romanization in use at the time of the novel. So, Nanking Road is Nanking Road and not Nanjing, and Chiang Kai-shek and Tu Yueh-sheng are used instead of Jiang Jieshi and Du Yuesheng.

The streets and places described are accurate to the best of my ability. The various cabarets, bars, and buildings in the text existed at the locations mentioned. The major historical events described, including the fighting between Japanese and Chinese forces, all occurred, although I have taken some liberties with the particulars, none of which change what actually took place.

The principal characters are fictional with the exception of Father Jacquinot, a truly remarkable man. His interaction with Jack Ford, however, is entirely fictional. Various historical personalities are mentioned, and when they are, I have tried to be true to their character if not to actual events. I have included thumbnail sketches of these remarkable people in the Notes on Characters.

A Glossary of Shanghai Terms

Bamboo Brit—A derogatory term. An American who adopts exaggerated British manners.

Bund—Indian word meaning embankment and the name for Shanghai's iconic waterfront.

Burlington Bertie—A Chinese who picks up cigarette butts and strips out the tobacco to roll and sell as a new cigarette.

Chit—An I.O.U., a promise to pay at the end of the month. Shanghailanders signed chits at the better places to avoid having to carry around large amounts of cash.

Coasters—A derogatory term for an unattached woman who is believed to be of loose morals, but not a prostitute.

Coppers—Small coins.

Hutong—A narrow lane or alley.

Inshallah—Arabic word meaning "If God is willing."

Pao-chia system—A system of organization dating from the Northern Sung Dynasty used to maintain order, collect taxes, and manage civil projects.

Ronin—Shanghai term for the thugs the Japanese used to intimate and terrorize. Originally a ronin was a samurai who had no master to follow.

Shanghailanders—Term foreign nationals working and living in Shanghai used to describe themselves.

Shroff — Person who made the rounds collecting payment for the chits.

Sonya — Derogatory term for a lower class White Russian woman.

Tiffin-Lunch.

Taipans and compradors — The heads of the large Western firms in Shanghai like Jardine Matheson and their Chinese counterparts.

About The Author

A China expert and former senior executive with the CIA, Martin Petersen has written widely on Asia and national security issues, and City of Lost Souls is his first novel. He lives in the Texas Hill Country, where he pursues his hobby — collecting books, maps, articles, and ephemera about old Shanghai, almost 500 items — usually with a Bombay Saphire martini nearby. Straight up with a twist and not too dry.